THE SEVENTH TOWER

AENIR

Also by Garth Nix

The Seventh Tower series

The Fall
Castle

The Old Kingdom series

Sabriel
Lirael
Abhorsen

Across the Wall

The Keys to the Kingdom series

Mister Monday
Grim Tuesday
Drowned Wednesday
Sir Thursday
Lady Friday
Superior Saturday

Other titles

The Ragwitch
Shade's Children

THE SEVENTH TOWER
AENIR

GARTH NIX

HarperCollins *Children's Books*

First published in the USA by Scholastic Inc 2001
First published in Great Britain by HarperCollins *Children's Books* 2009
HarperCollins *Children's Books* is a division of HarperCollins*Publishers* Ltd,
77-85 Fulham Palace Road, Hammersmith, London W6 8JB

www.harpercollins.co.uk

www.garthnix.co.uk

1

ISBN 978 0 00 726121 5

Printed and bound in England by
Clays Ltd, St Ives plc

Mixed Sources
Product group from well-managed
forests and other controlled sources
www.fsc.org   Cert no. SW-COC-1806
© 1996 Forest Stewardship Council

FSC is a non-profit international organisation established to promote the
responsible management of the world's forests. Products carrying the FSC
label are independently certified to assure consumers that they come
from forests that are managed to meet the social, economic and
ecological needs of present and future generations.

Find out more about HarperCollins and the environment at
www.harpercollins.co.uk/green

To the total Seventh Tower team:
All the people at Lucasfilm who have
worked so hard on publishing the books
and getting them to readers.

1

The mountain appeared to be one gigantic mass of grey stone looming over the green river valley.

But it was not really a mountain.

It was a creature of stone. Old and cold and enormous, it liked to lie in one place for thousands of years, sleeping and dreaming of the time it was born from the fiery depths of the earth.

Since it had sat in one place for so long, most travellers thought that it was a fixed and permanent part of the terrain. Unlike the rest of Aenir, where forests walked and hills wrestled and rivers changed their courses whenever they felt like it.

On their maps the Chosen of the Castle called the great hulk of rock Cold Stone Mountain. Every year the Chosen came from another world to Aenir and spent many weeks trapping and enslaving the local creatures to take back to their own place to serve as Spiritshadows.

But some of the Chosen knew that Cold Stone Mountain was not a mountain at all. One particular Chosen had even found out how to make the mountain move.

One day he had made Cold Stone Mountain stretch and rumble and lift itself out of the bed of lesser rock that formed the valley floor.

While the mountain creature arched its back two other Chosen – companions of the first – scuttled in, right under the massive belly of gold-flecked granite, and put something in one of the many holes and caverns that pockmarked Cold Stone Mountain's underside.

Unfortunately for those two Chosen, their master could not maintain the magic that made the mountain move. It settled back a little earlier than expected and the two men were crushed to death. The object they had put in the crevice survived, locked away in darkness under six hundred stretches of solid rock.

The object was almost indestructible. A single crystal that had been grown into a rectangular shape, it was about as high as a tall Chosen, three times as wide and only a hand span thick. Even without light its surface shone like water reflecting the moon, a mysterious silver luminosity.

Occasionally the light would ripple in a rainbow effect and there would be pictures, absolutely lifelike pictures, that moved on its strange surface. Or there might be writing in the elegant and complex script used by the Chosen, or the blocky runes of the Icecarls.

The strange, shining object was the Codex of the Chosen and its rightful place was in the Castle, atop the Mountain of Light in the Dark World. It did not belong in Aenir and should never have been brought there.

The Codex had many powers, but none that would help it burrow through stone or make the mountain creature move. All of its power lay in knowledge – gathering knowledge and giving knowledge.

Down in the deep dark of its rocky prison the Codex could only use one of its many powers. It could see and hear through the minds of animals, using them as its eyes and ears.

It started to seek out those minds as soon as the mountain that imprisoned it settled down.

In the first year the Codex found eyeless, deaf worms.

In the second year it found blind crickets that scuttled through the many cracks and fissures of the mountain.

In the third year the Codex found lumps of semi-intelligent mould, which had no senses at all that the magical artefact could understand.

For several years after that the Codex continued to send out its questing mental tendrils, only to encounter useless creatures... or nothing at all.

It was not in the Codex's nature to give up. It would keep trying for a hundred years, or a thousand.

Fortunately it did not have to. A mere twenty-two years after it was stolen from the Castle and placed under the mountain, it found a Grugel. The Codex had not personally encountered a Grugel before, but it knew exactly what one was when it felt the mind of the small armour-plated rodent. The Grugel had come down from outside to eat the blind crickets and now it was returning. It crossed the Codex's cave on its way to climb up a very narrow chimney, using the hooks on its legs and throwing its equally hooked tail ahead like a climbing rope.

The Codex entered the mind of the Grugel and went with it to the outside world. It could enter the minds of several thousand animal-level intelligences at once, or a single Aeniran creature of human intelligence, though this was very difficult. It could not enter the minds of actual humans. Its makers had prohibited that.

But the Codex had to be close to its first target, or be able to see out of one of its helper's eyes.

From the Grugel it entered the minds of a roving pair of Lipits and then a whole swarm of Frox. After that it kept adding eyes and ears from all sorts of creatures. Slowly the Codex's perception ranged over almost the whole of Aenir.

It was not a constant presence though. Sometimes creatures died or the Codex simply lost touch with them, as happened when they strayed too far from another one of the Codex's eyes and ears. The Codex had to constantly work at keeping the many thousands of minds in its unique spy network linked back to its dark prison.

Always the Codex hoped to see or hear someone ask the question it desperately wanted to answer: "Where is the Codex of the Chosen?" or "How can I find the Codex?"

Once the question was asked, the Codex could use one of the animals it controlled to guide the questioner or communicate with them.

But it was the nature of the Codex that it could only answer questions. It could not act of its own accord.

So the Codex brooded in its prison, watching the life of Aenir through the eyes of its many agents and listening through their many ears.

It most closely watched the Chosen, for they were its people. On the Day of Ascension it would send hundreds of creatures running, jumping, flying and burrowing towards the

Chosen Enclave, waiting for the people of the Castle to appear from the Dark World as they did every year.

The Codex knew that the Chosen were forbidden to come to Aenir before the Day of Ascension, but still some came. It watched these people with particular care. It had been brought to Aenir by Chosen who had crossed over before the Day.

The Codex didn't really feel human emotions – or so it told itself. But something very like excitement and wonder did ripple across its surface one rainy afternoon when one of its eyes, a flipper-footed, furry lozenge known as a Vabe, crawled out of a newly formed lake and up a hill.

Through the Vabe's eyes the Codex saw something that it did not expect. It was still two weeks until the Day of Ascension, but there were two Dark Worlders on the hill. A boy and a girl.

Even stranger, the boy was a Chosen and the girl one of the Ship Folk, who now called themselves Icecarls.

Acting on instructions from the Codex the Vabe crawled closer. It didn't want to because there was a lot of thunder and lightning about. But the Codex drove it on.

Soon the Codex learned the boy's name was Tal. The girl was Milla.

It watched as they performed some ceremony that they obviously thought was important. Halfway through, as they offered drops of blood to the storm above them, the Codex realised what was going to happen.

Most places in Aenir were layered with magic and old traditions bound into the land. This was one of them. Blood given on Hrigga Hill would call the Storm Shepherds to a gathering and they would perform a service for a price – a price that was always the same.

A life.

Sure enough there in the black clouds above were two Storm Shepherds. They would be forced to answer the call of blood, even if it was offered in ignorance.

It was too late to interfere. Besides what could the Codex do with a single Vabe? It was only as big as the boy's foot and couldn't even bite. Vabes chewed weeds. Very slowly.

The Storm Shepherds came down, giant humanlike figures made of dark cloud and lightning. The Codex listened as they demanded the life that the Chosen and the Icecarl had unknowingly promised them. It would have liked to enter the mind of the larger Storm Shepherd, but its link with the Vabe was too tenuous and the Codex knew it would not be able to make the connection. It would simply lose the Vabe.

All it could do was listen.

The Chosen and the Icecarl refused.

The Storm Shepherds raised their storm-cloud fists and lightning began to grow there, small sparks growing longer and longer. In a few seconds the Storm Shepherds would unleash the lightning bolts and blast the boy and girl off the hill.

A pang of hunger rippled through the Vabe. It hadn't eaten for an hour. The Codex tried to suppress the instinct to eat, to keep the animal focused on the Chosen boy and the Icecarl girl.

The Vabe's hunger grew stronger. The link wavered. The Codex's vision through the little animal blurred.

Then everything went black.

2

Rain swept the hill and lightning flickered all around it. Two small figures, a Chosen boy and an Icecarl girl, stood defiantly before the great cloud-creatures who towered over them.

"We demand a life!" roared the Storm Shepherds together, their voices as loud and blasting as a storm wind. "Who shall pay?"

"We won't give you anything!" Tal shouted as he raised his Sunstone ring. He focused his mind on it and it shone brighter and brighter as he prepared to unleash a blast of concentrated light at the Storm Shepherds.

At his side Milla raised her Merwin-horn sword.

She had a Sunstone too, but was not trained in its use. At least not yet. Tal hoped that her sword would be able to cut through the strange cloud-flesh of the Storm Shepherds as well as it cut through shadow back in the Castle.

"You called us!" the larger of the two Storm Shepherds boomed. "Called by blood on old Hrigga Hill, we must take what is offered and give you a gift in return."

Tal thought he heard an odd tone in the Storm Shepherd's voice. It sounded as if it didn't want to take a life, that it was being *forced* to claim one. He knew that many of the creatures of Aenir were bound by ancient spells, magic that the Chosen did not know. Perhaps these Storm Shepherds were subject to such a binding which made them take a life if blood was spilled on this particular hill.

"We didn't mean to call you," he shouted back. It was hard to talk with the wind howling around the hilltop and the constant spray of rain that came with it – not to mention the growling thunder of the Storm Shepherds and the crackle of the lightning in their hands.

"Yet call you did," roared the Storm Shepherd. It sounded almost sad.

As it spoke, it raised its hand higher still – and then suddenly threw a whole fistful of lightning at Tal and Milla!

"Ru—!" shouted Milla, but her warning was cut off as the lightning exploded at their feet. Icecarl and Chosen were blinded and stunned and then deafened as the thunderclap rolled round and round the hill.

Tal wasn't sure what happened next. He crawled around on all fours, fingers squelching in the mud. He tried to get up and face the attackers, to counterattack with blasts of light from his Sunstone. But he couldn't see or hear. He collided with Milla and they both fell on to their backs.

When Tal tried to get up he felt an overpowering force pushing him down into the mud, pressing on his chest and shoulders so it was hard to breathe. He struggled, but it was no use.

"Milla!" he shouted. His own voice echoed inside his head, but he couldn't seem to hear it through his ears. He couldn't use his Sunstone either, because he couldn't see it. He had to be able to see the light to focus and bend it to his will. Otherwise all he could do was make it glow.

If only he still had his shadowguard, he thought. It could have done something. But it was free now, free because he was old enough to bind his own Spiritshadow, to make one of the creatures of Aenir his servant, to cross back with him to the Castle and...

Old enough to bind a Spiritshadow...

Tal could try and bind the Storm Shepherd that was holding him down. He could make the creature serve him.

It might be the only way to save their lives. Even so Tal hesitated, thoughts flickering through his mind like the Storm Shepherd's lightning. He could only bind an Aeniran to be his Spiritshadow once. It would be the most important thing he ever did. His Spiritshadow would influence his position in the Castle, would help him rise to Violet or fall to Red.

He had always thought he'd look over many different Aeniran creatures before he made his choice. He would weigh up their advantages and disadvantages. Talk with his parents about which creature would be best. Discuss it with his friends.

Tal didn't even know what a Storm Shepherd Spiritshadow would be like. He'd never seen one, either in Aenir or in the Castle. Maybe they made really rotten Spiritshadows.

Only, if Tal didn't bind the Storm Shepherd he would probably die. Then there would be no one to save Gref, or his mother, or Kusi, or to find his father.

What would Rerem do? Tal asked himself.

Tal could almost hear his father answer, feel his grip as they clasped forearms in farewell.

Look after your mother and the children, Tal. I'm depending upon you.

Tal felt the beginning of a sob rise in his throat. He had failed so far. His mother, Graile, was in a coma. His brother, Gref, was a prisoner, taken by a Spiritshadow that Tal hoped the Codex would identify. His youngest sister, Kusi, was being fostered by his cousins, friends of Shadowmaster Sushin, Tal's declared enemy. His father, Rerem, was lost, the only clue to his fate a scratched name in an illegal prison pit back in the Castle.

Tal's mouth set in determination. He would not fail any more.

He would do whatever had to be done. His choice of Spiritshadow was nothing, though he couldn't help but feel a pang as he decided to give up a precious, long-cherished dream.

He would bind the Storm Shepherd.

But he had to be able to see.

Tal started to blink very quickly, hoping that would help. Surely he was only temporarily blinded? What if the Storm Shepherd killed him before he could see? But then, they only wanted one life...

The blinking did help. Slowly Tal's vision returned. Patches of fuzzy colour joined together and became sharper.

The Storm Shepherd was holding him down with just one cloudy finger. The other Storm Shepherd needed two of its three fingers to hold Milla down. Tal's arms and hands were free. He could see his Sunstone again, despite the constant rain and the howling wind that whipped around the Storm Shepherds. Off the hill it wasn't even raining.

Tal had practised binding Aeniran creatures for

many years. It was the culmination of all of a Chosen's child training when they bound a creature and brought it back to the Castle and the Dark World to serve them as a Spiritshadow. He knew all the spells and rituals by heart.

First he must Mark the Bounds. Then he had to Speak the Words. Finally they had to Share the Shadow.

He had never thought he would do any of these things while lying on his back with an all-too-solid Storm Shepherd's finger pressing him into the mud.

"Which one of you shall die?" roared the Storm Shepherds once again speaking in unison. This close their voices were deafening.

Tal answered, but not in words. Instead he raised his Sunstone ring. A narrow beam of orange light sprang out of it, going straight through the nearest Storm Shepherd. It didn't seem to notice, but the beam wasn't meant to harm anyway. It was a marker.

Tal quickly used the beam to draw a circle that included the two Storm Shepherds and Milla, as well as himself. Where the beam of light struck the ground the grass and mud took on an orange luminescence.

Constrained by the Storm Shepherd the circle was a bit wonky. Certainly it wouldn't have got Tal a pass mark back in the Lectorium. But it was a closed circle of light and so Tal had completed the first part of the Binding of a Spiritshadow. He had Marked the Bounds.

"What are you doing?" asked the Storm Shepherd. It didn't sound disturbed. Just curious. "You only need to decide which one of you is to die."

Now Tal spoke, but it was a spell that he chanted, not an answer. He did not know what the words meant, for he had been taught them by rote and they were not of a language used by the Chosen. Because of this he had practised Speaking the Words almost every day for years. Binding a Spiritshadow was the act that marked the beginning of his adult life, and the type and strength of the Spiritshadow he gained would greatly influence his ability to rise through the Orders of the Castle.

Tal suppressed a sudden image of himself trailing through the Red Corridors, while everyone laughed behind their hands, whispering, "Look at his Spiritshadow. He bound a Storm Shepherd, can you believe it?"

"Mestrel ol Tel, Asteyr, Mestrel ol Lameth, amsal gebborn yeo nebedi—"

"What are you doing!" Milla shrieked. She threw herself forward so violently that the Storm Shepherd holding her had to use its third and last finger to bring her under control. "You can't say that!"

"What!" exclaimed Tal, shocked by the sudden outburst. In that moment, he lost track of the spell. The words had to be said exactly, without pause. He had felt the power building in them and had *known* he would be able to bind the Storm Shepherd. Now as the power of the words dissipated, the bounds faded too.

Milla had spoiled his one chance to bind the Storm Shepherd. If he'd managed it, he could have set his new servant against the other Storm Shepherd. They wouldn't have to choose who had to die.

"You've ruined it!" Tal shouted. He tried to roll over to Milla, but the cloud finger held him fast.

"Ruined what?" asked Milla angrily. "How did you learn the Crones' Talk?"

"You have to decide," interrupted the smaller Storm Shepherd. "One of you has to die—"

"Shut up!" Tal yelled. Surprisingly the Storm Shepherd did. "What do you mean Crones' Talk? I was Speaking the Words. I was trying to bind the Storm Shepherd and save your stupid life!"

"It was Crones' Talk, the Old Tongue," insisted Milla. "The Prayer to Asteyr, which can only be said by a Crone Mother. It is forbidden to everyone else."

"How do you know that's what I was saying?" asked Tal.

The two Storm Shepherds nodded, as if he'd asked a good question.

"I have heard it," said Milla, her voice low. "Five times. The last was only a half-circling ago when Olof Snowswimmer slew Ifrim No-Nose in his sleep. Olof would not accept the judgment of the Crone Mother and she had to say the prayer."

"What happened?" growled the smaller Storm Shepherd. All the lightning that it had held in its hand was gone now and its eyes sparked more brightly.

"The Crone Mother called on Asteyr and she

made Olof walk into the Living Sea," said Milla. "He was not crushed by the Selski, but caught on a fluke and dragged for many stretches across the Ice before he died."

Tal was silent. *Asteyr* was one of the words in the binding spell, repeated several times. But how could the Chosen's binding spell be the same as the Icecarls Prayer to Asteyr?

"This is all very interesting," grumbled the larger Storm Shepherd. "But you still have to decide. Which of you is to die?"

3

As the Storm Shepherd finished speaking, Milla suddenly struck at the one holding her down, plunging her bone knife into the creature's middle finger. The knife sank hilt-deep into the cloud-flesh and then bounced out again, the cloud reforming.

"Don't do that," said the Storm Shepherd. "It tickles."

Milla slid her knife back into her sleeve and took a deep breath.

"I will be the one to die," she announced. "But only if Tal promises to take my Sunstone to the Far Raiders, and tell the Crone Mother of the Ship everything I have seen."

"Hold on!" said Tal. He'd been thinking about the Storm Shepherds' curious reluctance to actually go ahead and kill one of them. "I don't think either of us has to die."

"Blood has been offered on Old Hrigga Hill!" roared the larger Storm Shepherd. "A life must be given and a gift granted. The girl has offered her life and we will take it!"

"No, take mine," said Tal quickly. "I'm offering as well. But only if Milla helps find the Codex and takes it back to Ebbitt so he can find Gref."

"Two lives..." muttered the larger Storm Shepherd. It sounded confused. "This is not the way of things. One life, one gift. That is the rule of the hill."

"What if we don't ask for a gift?" questioned Tal. "Say we gave *you* a gift instead of a life?"

"No," grumbled the Storm Shepherd, shaking its head. "Never before has this happened on Old Hrigga Hill. One life is taken, one gift given!"

"I would like a gift, Adras," said the other Storm Shepherd. "No one has ever given us a gift."

"There is no choice, Odris," said the larger

Storm Shepherd. "We are bound to the hill and must serve its wants."

"Adras and Odris," said Milla. "I am Milla of the Far Raiders and that is Tal."

"Of the Chosen," added Tal. The pressure on his chest was lightening. The Storm Shepherds obviously found it harder to crush people they'd been introduced to.

Now that he knew their names, Tal could see differences between the two Storm Shepherds. Adras was taller by several stretches and wider, and had more lightning running along its puffy arms and hands. Odris was slighter and there were many more sparks in its eyes. From their shapes, Tal could tell Adras was male and Odris female.

"One must die," repeated Adras. He was stuck on that.

"But we have to decide, don't we?" asked Tal. "That's the nature of the binding, isn't it?"

Tal knew that the great majority of the creatures of Aenir were bound to particular places, or to follow certain paths, or to roam within severely limited boundaries. Within these bounds, they were also constrained to follow age-old spells and rituals.

If Tal could work out the exact nature of the binding he might be able to save himself and Milla.

Adras didn't answer, but Tal saw Odris wink.

"Let us up so we can talk about it," said Tal. "After all, you can catch us if we try to run away."

The Storm Shepherds looked at each other. Then they lifted their hands and billowed back. Tal and Milla stood up and wiped the mud off their bodies. Most of it was on their backs. After a moment's hesitation they helped each other get the worst of it off.

"Now, let me get this straight," said Tal. "You two are bound to this hill. If blood is spilled here then you must come and ask for a life and give a gift in return."

"So it has always been," rumbled Adras.

"Since the Forgetting," added Odris.

"The Forgetting?" asked Tal, curious. "What was that?"

"We do not know," replied Odris. "There is only the time before the Forgetting, which we do not know, and the time after, which we do."

"How is this going to help us?" whispered Milla to Tal. "Blind them with your Sunstone and we will run. They have said they are bound here. Once off the hill we will be safe."

"Their lightning isn't bound," Tal whispered back. "If we run they'll probably roast us both."

"No whispering!" ordered Adras. He was getting impatient again. "Which one will die?"

"If you weren't bound to this hill you wouldn't have to take a life, would you?" asked Tal.

His question surprised the Storm Shepherds. Thunder crackled around them and they bowed their heads together. They obviously thought their whispers could not be heard, but even whispering their voices were as loud as a human speaking normally.

"Freedom?"

"Can he free us?"

"What will Hrigga do?"

"I can free you," announced Tal. "Sort of anyway."

He hesitated before he continued. What he said next would seal his future and could not be unsaid.

"How?" boomed Adras. "How?"

"You will have to volunteer to become our Spiritshadows," Tal blurted out. He felt sick knowing that he was giving up the future he'd dreamed about, of a dragon Spiritshadow like the Empress's, or a majestic maned cat like Ebbitt's. That made him feel guilty too. How could he even temporarily value that more than Gref's freedom or his mother's life?

He'd also forgotten what it would mean to Milla.

"What!" exploded Milla. She looked at Tal as if he had suddenly turned into a Merwin. "I cannot have a Spiritshadow!"

"It's the only thing I can think of," explained Tal wretchedly. "Great-uncle Ebbitt told me once about an Aeniran creature who *volunteered* to be a Spiritshadow, instead of being forced. It bound itself freely to a Chosen and so became free of the bonds that held it to a place. Of course the Chosen who let it wasn't allowed to bring it back until it was rebound to be an actual servant, not a companion... anyway, if they volunteer we don't have to Mark the Bounds or Speak the Words. We just Share the Shadow, which means giving them our natural shadows—"

"My shadow?" asked Milla, her voice as cold as the ice she came from. Her hand was on the hilt of her Merwin-horn sword. "We have shared much, Tal of the Chosen. But do not think you have made me like you. I will not give up my shadow. I would rather die."

Tal shook as he held back angry words. He couldn't believe Milla was being so stubborn. Everything depended on this. Their own lives. His whole family.

Besides, he was honouring her, giving her the opportunity to get a Spiritshadow, to become almost like a Chosen!

He turned back to the Storm Shepherds, but Odris forestalled his next question.

"Both of us must be freed from the hill. You must take both of us to be Spiritshadows."

Milla shook her head.

Tal stared at her. Their eyes met, but neither Chosen nor Icecarl blinked. It was a test of wills. Tal was sure that asking the Storm Shepherds to voluntarily join them as Spiritshadows was the only way to avoid either himself or Milla being sacrificed.

They were still staring when the ground beneath their feet suddenly shook, dropping at least a stretch. Tal and Milla both fell over again. Milla went over backwards and struck her head on a stone.

"Hrigga wakes!" roared Adras. "We accept your offer!"

He reached forwards and placed his hand around Tal's shadow, as if he would pick it up. But he did not close his fingers. Odris did the same to Milla's shadow. Tal expected the Icecarl to protest or move away, but Milla had struck her head sharply. She groggily tried to sit up, but her shadow didn't move enough to evade Odris's grasp.

Both Storm Shepherds paused. The ground continued to quake under Tal's feet and he saw thin cracks suddenly run through the mud. Then they grew wider and joined until one huge crack ran under Tal and Milla.

"Light!" boomed Odris. "We cannot take your shadows without your light!"

Tal tore his attention away from the quickly widening crack under him. It was opening like a mouth, to swallow him up. He looked at Milla for an instant – and made his decision.

Look after your mother and the children, Tal. I'm depending upon you.

He raised his Sunstone above his head and called the light that was used in the final part of a Spiritshadow binding, the light that moved through all seven colours, the light that shared the shadow.

In that strange rainbow flicker, both his and Milla's shadows appeared more solid, more real. The Storm Shepherds picked them up and thrust them into the middle of their cloud-bodies, where their hearts would be if they had them.

Tal felt a wrench as his shadow disappeared and a rush of cold air that seemed to pass through his head. Immediately he became more aware of the amount of moisture in the air, and of the wind and sky. Small sparks shot out of his fingers and around his Sunstone. On the ground, Milla was also briefly surrounded by crackling sparks.

Then the hill split completely in two revealing a deep, dark abyss.

Tal teetered on the edge, flailing his arms as he tried to regain his balance. Milla, still half-unconscious, slid over the edge in a fountain of loose dirt, mud and stone.

Both fell into the dark earth.

4

As Tal and Milla fell the Storm Shepherds dived after them. Swooping down, they grabbed their new companions and shot back out of the crevasse. Just as they cleared the rim the giant crack snapped shut, spraying earth, stones and mud into the sky.

"Free!" boomed Adras as he rose up into the sky, Tal dangling from one puffy hand. "Free!"

"Free!" sang Odris. "Free at last, of the hateful hill!"

"Well, not exactly," shouted Tal. "You are Spiritshadows after all. Or you will be when we get back to the Castle."

He wasn't sure what the procedure was now.

If he'd bound Adras to him in the usual way, the Storm Shepherd would be a servant and would have to do what he was told. But he was a free companion.

Somehow, Tal thought, every time he got himself out of trouble he created a whole lot more for himself as well. Nothing was ever simple.

Thinking of trouble made Tal look across at Milla. She was hanging limply in Odris's grip, clearly still dazed by the blow to her head.

"And you are my Chosen," answered Adras, which made Tal frown. "Where do we travel, Tal?"

"Down for a start," said Tal, suppressing a shiver. They'd gone up a long way very quickly and it was cold. Old Hrigga Hill was far below them, with the new lake surrounding it. He could see the forest, the one where the trees had walked away. They had stopped on higher ground quite a long way south.

The sun was almost down now. It had settled behind the line of hills to the west. The stars were quite clear above the hills gleaming in the constellations of Aenir, many of them familiar to Tal from his early childhood. His family had always spent their first night in Aenir after the Day of Ascension looking at the stars. There was the many-starred cluster called the Jewel Box and the triangular formation known as the Dragonhead, though Tal didn't think it really looked like one.

They reminded him of his family – so far away, beyond his grasp.

It was easy to keep staring at the stars, but that would not help his mission. Tal looked away. He had to think of what to do next. He had to forget about his lost Spiritshadow and focus on finding the Codex.

The Codex would help him find Gref. Gref was the first step towards reuniting his family.

One step at a time.

"Adras has not left the bounds since the Forgetting and I have been bound all my life," said Odris, gliding closer and interrupting Tal's thoughts. "It is strange to do more than look upon distant lands. Where shall we alight?"

Tal peered down. There was the lake, the forest and wide patches of bare grassland. He could see a ring of standing stones, but that was probably best avoided, for strong magic and stronger creatures made such places their home.

There were also some low hills, but Tal didn't like the look of them, after his experience with Old Hrigga. That was the trouble with Aenir, he thought. You could never tell when a hill was just a hill.

"How about there?" he asked, pointing to an area of burnt-out grassland. It looked like a fire had raced through within the last few days. Hopefully this meant that the earth was just earth and anything else that might have lurked there would have fled the fire.

The Storm Shepherds began to drop down. Tal noticed that Adras got quite a lot colder as they fell and that he kept looking across at Odris and adjusting his rate of fall to match her speed.

Tal sighed. It was already clear that Adras – who would be his Spiritshadow back in the Castle – was not the smartest of Storm Shepherds. Big and powerful, but a bit of a Dimmer when it came to brainpower. It was even worse than he feared. A smart Spiritshadow was of enormous help to an ambitious Chosen. A stupid one was quite the reverse.

"Milla? Are you all right?" Tal called out as Adras dropped him the last few stretches down on the blackened earth. The fire had been recent, because he could still smell it. The odour of burnt grass was very strong.

Odris hovered even lower than Adras and gently lay Milla down. The Icecarl didn't move.

Tal hurried over. Milla must have hit her head harder than he'd thought. He knelt down beside her and mentally ran over the healing spells he could cast with his Sunstone. But if she had a really serious head injury there was nothing—

Suddenly he found himself on his back, with Milla's knee on his chest and her bone knife at his throat. She leaned close, her eyes wild and her mouth set in an animal snarl.

"Traitor!" she shouted and dug the point of her knife into his neck, hard enough to draw a thin trickle of blood. "You sold my shadow!"

"But we had to—" Tal tried to say. Milla was really going to kill him this time, he suddenly knew. The knife hurt and she would need to slide it in only a little bit more.

"I *should* kill you," hissed Milla. "Shadow-stealer!"

She returned the knife to her sleeve. Tal sighed in relief. But his sigh was cut off as Milla suddenly pushed her thumbs against two nerves on his neck. She pushed quickly three times. On the third push Tal's eyes closed and his head fell back.

Milla stood up. The two Storm Shepherds looked at her.

"I suppose I should defend my companion," said Adras, looking down at Tal's unconscious form. "I felt that too you know."

"But then you would have to fight me, brother," said Odris.

Adras shrugged. "He seems to be unhurt."

"Give me back my shadow!" Milla screamed. She drew her Merwin-horn sword and cut at Odris, but the sword just went straight through the cloud-flesh. The bright Merwin horn could cut shadow, but here in Aenir, Odris was not a shadow.

"I can't," said Odris plaintively. "We are tied together now, until the end of our days. I will go with you to your—"

"No! No! No!" screamed Milla, hacking away at

the Storm Shepherd. But her furious blows only exhausted her. Odris bore them without flinching. Adras merely watched Tal, crouching at his side like a huge statue carved from fog.

Finally Milla stood back and took several very slow breaths. She was using a Rovkir exercise to prevent the onset of berserk fury.

"You'll get used to it," said Odris.

"No I won't," said Milla. "I will give myself to the Ice."

"There isn't much Ice on Aenir," said Odris. "There might not be any. It's a hot place on the whole—"

"I will return to the Dark World," Milla stated coldly. "I will find the Chosen Enclave and force one of them to show me how to cross back. Then I will give myself to the Ice."

"Why?" asked Odris.

Milla stood staring into space for a moment then she whispered, "I cannot be an Icecarl without my shadow. I cannot be a Shield Maiden without my shadow. I am no one without my shadow."

"But I'll be your shadow when we—" Odris started to say. Before the Storm Shepherd could continue Milla turned and ran out into the star-flecked darkness.

Odris sighed, a big sigh that swept up a cloud of charcoal dust that blew over Adras. He growled and puffed himself up a few times to shake it off.

"I have to go after her," said Odris. She sounded a bit surprised. "It feels very odd to be bound to a person rather than to a place."

"It does, doesn't it?" agreed Adras. "I hope mine wakes up soon."

"I will try to bring mine back," said Odris. "Make sure you tell the wind where you are, Adras, so I can find you. And don't go across to the Dark World without me."

"I will – won't," replied Adras. "I mean, I will tell the wind and I won't cross."

The two Storm Shepherds slowly billowed their arms out to touch palms. Then Odris leapt up into the sky. She drew the wind around her and set off after Milla.

Adras sat back down and looked at Tal. Somehow he could feel that the boy was all right. He was only sleeping now.

It *was* odd being bound to a person, Adras thought, as his own breathing matched Tal's, and he felt his lightning-charged eyes begin to close. Storm Shepherds rarely slept, but he felt like it now.

As his eyes closed his body lost its form, arms and legs spreading till they joined. The dark, threatening cloud in his middle smoothed into fluffy white.

Within minutes Adras became a circular mass of low cloud, hovering above the sleeping Tal.

Out in the darkness three creatures looked upon the sleeping boy and considered what he might be like to eat. Tongues flicked in and out, sampling the air. There was a bitter tang to it, something to do with the cloud. Something that hinted of danger.

The creatures hesitated. Perhaps the sleeping Chosen was not the easy prey they sought. They touched tongues, exchanging information. Together they would decide whether to attack... or not.

5

Milla fled through the darkness. But it was not the darkness she knew. There were tiny lights in the sky, stars, as Tal called them. There were unfamiliar scents in the air. Strange sounds, the calls of creatures that she did not know.

She didn't even know which direction she was running in. It was an unusual feeling for her. She had never been lost on the Ice, not for an instant. There was always a smell, a sound, the texture of the ice, the direction of the wind or the Selski migration.

There was always *something*. Now there was nothing to tell her where she was.

Milla was lost in a strange land. Another world.

She had lost her shadow and with it, her future.

She had always wanted to be a Shield Maiden, dedicating her life to all the clans and the protection of all Icecarls. Free-willed shadows were one of the things the Shield Maidens swore to protect their people from.

Back in the Dark World Odris would be just such a shadow. Milla could never return to her people with Odris.

But perhaps, she thought, if she could get back to the Dark World and the Ruin Ship without Odris following, the Mother Crone would be able to get her normal shadow back.

Milla scowled. Here she was in a strange world and she was distracting herself with dreams that could not be.

Her duty was clear. Return to the Dark World, deliver the Sunstone ring to her clan, report to the Mother Crone and give herself to the Ice.

Something rustled ahead of her and Milla froze. She had no idea what it could be. There didn't seem to be anything there, but she was sure she'd heard something. The starlight was bright enough to see a silhouette at least – unless whatever made the noise was lying on the ground.

Milla drew her sword and advanced slowly. The glow of the Merwin horn was enough to light up the ground under her feet, but no further. She halted every few steps to listen and look carefully ahead of her.

There was nothing to see. The burned grassland had stopped twenty or thirty stretches behind her. Now there was just short green and yellow grass ahead. Too short to hide a creature bigger than Milla's foot.

Milla took a few more steps forwards. Something didn't feel quite right, but she wasn't sure what it was. There was a faint smell, something different than the burned patches or the usual smell of the grass.

She sniffed experimentally. The smell was close. It was the scent of slightly rotting meat, overlaid by the fresh scent of grass.

It was very close. Milla looked at the Sunstone ring on her hand. She didn't really know how to use it, but she thought she could probably raise some sort of light. Tal and Ebbitt had shown her how to concentrate on the stone.

The ground rippled slightly under her feet. Milla frowned. She still couldn't see anything in this starlight and she didn't know what she was smelling.

It was time to risk a light.

She raised her hand so she could look directly at the Sunstone. It reflected the starlight, but there was also the faintest hint of yellow fire at its centre. Milla stared at it, willing it to grow brighter.

It did start to grow brighter. Milla smiled. She could feel it in the middle of her forehead and could think it brighter. So she did.

It grew brighter still until she couldn't see her hand for the brightness. It was a harsh light, very different from the soft illumination of Icecarl moth-lamps.

Milla raised her hand above her head and looked around. She still couldn't see anything threatening. The only oddity was that she was standing on a large, irregular square of grass that was greener than all the rest...

Even as she saw that Milla realised this was more than odd.

She jumped forwards just as the Hugthing writhed up from the ground, wrapping its flat, mossy body round her legs and waist like a blanket.

Milla fell forwards. If she hadn't jumped she would have been totally smothered by the Hugthing. But even with her arms and head free the creature held her in a grip that was too strong to escape. Milla kicked and struck at it with her sword, but the moss simply absorbed the blows and tightened even more.

Desperately Milla lunged forwards and bit the Hugthing. Her teeth couldn't tear the moss.

The Hugthing squeezed tighter and Milla felt her muscles being crushed as she tried to resist. It was climbing up her stomach too and would soon have a grip on her lungs.

She had to do something.

Fire was probably the only thing that could hurt it. Milla suddenly realised that someone had tried to burn this monstrosity back where Tal and the

Storm Shepherds were. That was why there was a trail of burnt grassland.

Milla pushed her Sunstone against the moss and focused all her will on it, instinctively falling into the correct Rovkir-breathing pattern to shut off the pain of being crushed.

This time she wanted heat as well as light. She wanted the Sunstone to burn as hot as its namesake. Even if she lost her ring finger, she would escape this terrible living trap.

The Sunstone grew brighter and brighter, so bright that Milla had to half close her eyes and turn away.

But the stone didn't get any hotter and the Hugthing squeezed and squeezed. Milla felt her joints cracking and the air slowly being forced from her lungs...

6

There was a sudden rush of cold air above Milla. A cloud blotted out the stars and then a jagged bolt of lightning lit up the sky. It struck the green moss-back of the Hugthing and Milla felt a strange shock go through her body. The creature reared back, let out a high whistle and immediately let go of Milla. More lightning struck and thunder boomed. Milla crawled rapidly away. Her legs and ribs hurt, but as far as she could tell nothing was broken. She was just bruised and that was nothing to an Icecarl.

Above her head Odris sent down a dozen more lightning bolts, driving the Hugthing further away.

But even though it rippled and undulated across the ground at a frightful speed, it didn't seem badly hurt. It was clearly afraid of the lightning and each strike did leave a blackened mark on its green moss-back, but that was all.

Milla watched it flowing off and shuddered. Something that hard to slay was very dangerous indeed. At least she knew the smell of it now. Fresh-cut grass mixed with rotting meat.

She hoped she had a flaming torch and a bottle of Selski oil in her hand next time she saw one.

Odris sent one last bolt of lightning after the Hugthing, then circled back and settled down near Milla, growing two long legs to anchor herself in one place.

"I thank you," said Milla grudgingly.

"It was nothing," Odris replied modestly. "A Hugthing is no danger to me, of course. But they are vicious hunters of anything made of... meat."

"A Hugthing," said Milla, feeling along her legs to make certain they were only bruised. "It is well-named."

"Can I come with you now?" asked Odris. "I can help you."

"I can't stop you," said Milla bitterly. It had been a mistake coming to Aenir. She should have tried harder to leave the Castle and deliver the Sunstone to her clan. Now there was a chance she might not be able to get back at all and the Far Raiders would soon have nothing but moth-lamps and glowjellies to light their way.

Her chances of returning would be better if she let Odris help her. She hadn't properly thought everything through before. She'd panicked – something she never thought she'd do.

Milla frowned and forced herself to go back and think the problem through from the beginning.

Her quest was to deliver a Sunstone to the Far Raiders. She had forgotten that, letting herself imagine even greater triumphs, returning to the Ship with information even the Crone Mothers did not know. She had wanted to be a famous Shield Maiden, the one who had gone to another world and learned of new dangers to the clans.

That ambition had led her from her duty.

Neglect of her true purpose had destroyed her dream of being a Shield Maiden. She had wagered her future and had lost her shadow, all for pride and ambition. She had demonstrated to the world – and to herself – that she was not fit to be a Shield Maiden.

She knew she had to get back as soon as possible, deliver the Sunstone and then... the Ice would judge her.

So she *should* let Odris help her, at least for now.

"Where is the Chosen Enclave?" Milla asked. "Do you know?"

"I have heard travellers speak of it, and Chosen who have come to our hill to offer lives in exchange for gifts," said Odris. "I think it lies far to the north and east."

"How far?"

"Many days for me, even upon the wind," said Odris. "I can carry you for a while each day, but my strength is not great enough to do more."

"Which way is east?" asked Milla slowly. She hated not knowing directions.

"That way." Odris extended her arm to point.

"You see the bright star, halfway up the sky that is all alone? The one that shines a little blue? That is Norrin, sad star of the east, who weeps for company."

"What? How can it weep? Why is it blue?"

"It is only a story!" Odris laughed. "Stars are distant suns. I do not know why that one is blue. But Norrin always shows the way east."

"I do not understand stars," said Milla. "We do not have them."

"Ah, I have heard of the Veil," said Odris. "That must be strange to live always in darkness."

Milla was silent. The Dark World was not strange to her, but for the first time she wondered why it was so. The Veil was not a natural thing. It had been made, placed in the heavens to block out the light. Who had made it? And why?

"I will sleep now," said Milla. "Will you watch? I will count my breaths and wake when it is my turn."

"Sleep your fill!" encouraged Odris. "Storm Shepherds rarely sleep. We have long dozed above and around Old Hrigga Hill, so I am rested. Sleep!"

"The Hugthing has gone, hasn't it?" asked Milla.

She made her Sunstone brighten and carefully examined the grass all around. It was satisfactorily brown and uneven, but she still felt a faint buzz of fear as she lay down. It was odd to sleep without heavy furs, but the night was warm.

Milla made sure her sword was under her hand and then she began the process of telling herself to wake up after fourteen hundred breaths.

That done, she sank quickly into sleep.

Odris yawned, surprising herself. To keep awake, she launched herself into the air. She hadn't expected to feel sleepy, but it made sense. She could feel Milla's shadow inside her and the connection from it to the sleeping Icecarl.

Odris could also sense some part of Milla's dreams. It was like seeing something out of the corner of her eyes. She kept getting fleeting glimpses of a great expanse of ice and strange creatures and men and women in furs and a ship...

Odris blinked again, shutting the images out. Then she shot round in a wide circle, exerting herself in order to keep awake. There was no sign of the Hugthing, but there were many creatures that roamed the night in Aenir. Odris kept some lightning crackling in her right hand and her eyes on the ground.

She must not fall asleep. Her companion was counting on her.

7

Tal woke to find Adras floating above him, blocking out the sun. Judging from the heat and how high the sun was, it was late morning. Tal looked around at the grass blowing in the light breeze and sighed.

His neck hurt. There was no sign of Milla, or the other Storm Shepherd, Odris.

Perhaps there was something else he could have done Tal thought as he massaged his neck. But he couldn't think of anything, even now. Besides what was done was done.

The important thing was to move on. To find the Codex, which would lead him to Gref.

But he couldn't help thinking about Milla.

"I had to do it," he protested aloud, reassuring himself. "I had to do it."

The more he thought about it the more convinced he was that he'd been absolutely right and Milla was merely a barbarian who didn't understand.

She had no right to try and strangle him. After all the things he'd done for her. She had a Sunstone. Now she would have a Spiritshadow as well. She was practically a Chosen and she owed it all to Tal. Her silly Icecarl superstitions weren't worth bothering about.

He supposed she was an enemy now. If he saw her again he'd have to blast her before she could attack him.

He wished he hadn't thought of that. His anger melted away and he felt depressed. And hungry.

Still rubbing his neck, Tal walked out into the sun. Its heat cheered him up a little. He reminded himself that what he had to do *now* was work out where to go and what to do.

He had to forget about Milla and get on with finding the Codex.

A large flying beetle, all blue and gold, buzzed up and Tal brushed it away from his face. As he did so he saw part of the Storm Shepherd's shadow move. There was an area there that was darker in the outline of a boy. Tal moved his hand again and that darker shadow moved too.

Tal had not been taught about this in the Lectorium. He walked a few paces further away and moved his arms up and down. The darker boy-shadow in the middle of the Storm Shepherd's shadow moved its arms up and down.

Tal walked even further away, but the boy-shadow stayed exactly in the middle of Adras's shadow. It mimicked his movements, but did not follow him as a real shadow would.

Tal shook his head. There was so much to try and understand. Only a few months ago he had thought he knew pretty much everything he needed to know. He had supposed he was well on the way to becoming a Shadowmaster.

Now he only knew how much he didn't know.

"Hey, Adras!" he shouted. "I want to talk to you."

The cloud shivered and then started to reform

into man-shape again. It grew darker and lightning began to flicker in the shape of eyes. It took a few minutes to completely regain its form, then the Storm Shepherd bobbed a few stretches away from Tal.

"Were you asleep?" asked Tal.

"No!" exclaimed Adras, but he spoiled his answer by stretching his arms above his head and yawning, a yawn that sent a blast of cold air across Tal. "I was keeping watch."

"Sure," said Tal. "What happened to Milla and Odris?"

"They left," said Adras.

"I can see that," said Tal. "Where did they go?"

Adras shrugged and yawned again.

"Brilliant," muttered Tal. "I don't suppose you know anything about the Codex of the Chosen?"

"The what?" Adras swatted at the beetle that had suddenly returned. His huge hand narrowly missed Tal, who was blown back a step by the sudden rush of air.

"Careful!" shouted Tal. He walked back a few stretches and started again.

"The Codex of the Chosen. It's some sort of book. It can answer all sorts of questions. Have you heard of it, or where it might be?"

Adras scratched his head, small lightning flickering across his scalp. The beetle circled Tal's head, almost as if it was listening.

"No," Adras said finally. "Odris is the one to ask. She knows a lot."

"But we don't know where she's gone to," said Tal, keeping his temper in check. "Is there anyone else around who might be able to answer my questions? Is there anyone who can help me find the Codex?"

Adras raised one hand and rested his chin upon it, deep in thought. The beetle flew around Tal's head the other way and then made a series of strange up and down movements that Tal ignored.

"I suppose we could—" said Adras and stopped.

"Suppose what?" asked Tal.

"Follow Odris?" Adras suggested hopefully.

"But we don't know where she went." Tal was starting to feel very cross.

"I don't know where Odris went, but I can find

her," said Adras eagerly. "She will whisper to the wind and it will tell me."

"And you think Odris will know something about the Codex?" Tal was a little distracted by the blue and gold bug that had been flying so strangely. Now there were two bugs and then a third flew in, followed by a fourth. They were flying into a pattern right in front of his face.

"She might," said Adras. "Odris always talked to visitors more than I did."

Tal was no longer really listening. More and more bugs had flown in, and now they were landing on the burnt ground at his feet and moving into a very deliberate pattern.

Tal looked down at it perplexed. Fifty or sixty bugs had formed an arrow pointing southeast and there were at least as many building up some sort of symbol next to the arrow.

The symbol was about three-quarters formed when Tal realised what it was. A letter of the alphabet the Chosen used for Light Magic. The letter C.

"C!" said Tal. "Is that C for Codex?"

"What?" asked Adras. He leaned forwards to look

at the bugs. Unfortunately his breath blew half of them away, just as they were forming another letter, obviously in answer to Tal's question. It looked like a Y, but the bugs were blown away before it could be finished.

Tal took a very deep breath.

"What?" asked Adras again, puzzled. The bugs weren't doing anything organised now. They were crawling around aimlessly, or taking wing to disappear in all directions.

"It was a message," said Tal. He pointed in the direction the temporary arrow of bugs had indicated. "We're going this way."

"But Odris is in that direction," said Adras, pointing more north than east.

Tal hesitated. He had no way of knowing who had sent the bugs or how it was done. But finding the Codex was everything. With it he could find out who held his brother, Gref, captive and a lot more besides.

He looked down at the scars on his wrist, the marks of the oaths he had sworn with Milla. Then he deliberately pulled his sleeves down over them and started walking.

8

Milla woke exactly as she had ordered herself, on the exhalation of her fourteen-hundredth breath.

Night was ending and the sun was starting to rise. Milla stared at it in fascination. It really was like a gigantic Sunstone climbing above the hills.

"Thank the sky you're awake," said Odris. "I've been so sleepy."

Milla looked across at the Storm Shepherd. It was not so bad now, but every time she looked she imagined what the creature would be like as a shadow.

"You may rest," she said curtly. "I will watch."

"Oh, I'm not tired now," said Odris. "It's just that with the bond between us—"

"There is no bond!" said Milla angrily. "Or if there is, it is a false one."

Odris didn't answer. She simply flew off a short distance to give Milla more space.

Milla did some stretches, ignoring the pain from her bruises. In the light of day she saw that her legs were mottled with dark patches and scratches. There would be swelling too, in her joints. It would not be easy for her to walk.

But she didn't need to now that she had decided to use the Storm Shepherd to help her.

"Odris!" she called. The Storm Shepherd drifted closer.

"Pick me up," Milla ordered, holding up her arms. "We will fly to the closest water. I need to drink and wash."

Odris reached down and gripped Milla's forearms with her puffy fingers. Then she rose up in a series of jerks, trailing Milla only a few stretches above the ground.

They headed east, but Odris could not lift Milla

very high. Every now and then she actually dropped down far enough that Milla's feet touched, which hurt since they were flying quite fast. Milla noticed that Odris seemed able to change the wind so it always blew behind her, driving in the direction the Storm Shepherd chose.

The grassland continued for a long time. Odris started to dip more often and Milla's feet got quite sore, until finally they saw a small lake ahead. Bright blue, it glittered in the morning sun, an irregular patch of water about as big as a full-grown Selski and much the same shape.

"Set me down," Milla demanded.

Once again, Odris complied without speaking. She dropped Milla gently enough, right by the water's edge, then shot sharply up to rest fifty stretches or more above the Icecarl.

Milla looked at the water carefully. In her world open water was rare and very dangerous. Apart from a few permanent areas near hot springs it only occurred where the living sea of the Selski met the Slepenish that came up through the ice. The result of that encounter was always a vast swath of broken ice and choppy seas.

This water was very clear. Milla could see right down to its sandy bottom. She could see no sign of any fish, but there were small clumps of weeds.

Even so Milla was cautious. She drew her Merwin-horn sword. Keeping it in her right hand, she knelt down to dip her left hand in the lake and take a drink of water.

As her fingers touched the surface the water suddenly frothed and a current began to swirl violently around the edges. Milla snatched her hand back and retreated, sword at the ready.

The water continued to swirl. Then a huge shape suddenly rose out of the middle of the lake. For a moment Milla thought it was something like a Merwin emerging. Then she saw that it was actually more water, but water that had risen in a definite shape.

A second later Milla realised that it was a nose. And there were two deep black holes that were eyes and ridges of eyebrows made of darker, greener water.

The water from the lake had formed a giant face.

The mouth was only a few stretches away from where Milla had knelt. It opened. Water pushed up to form lips and drained away at the same time to create a throat.

The lips moved and a gurgling roar came out, accompanied by a fine spray that splashed over Milla. She winced and drew back. It took her a while to recognise that the gurgle was actually speech and that she could understand it.

"Who is it comes to take my blood?"

Milla didn't answer. She started to back away. This was all too reminiscent of Hrigga Hill and the Storm Shepherd's Challenge.

As she backed away her left hand suddenly thrust itself forwards without her control. Milla grimaced as the jolt ran through into her shoulder. It felt like her hand was held by an invisible rope, but all she could see were a few drops of water where she'd dipped it in the lake.

"Who comes, who comes to drink my blood?" said the face in the water. "Do you seek to leave so soon?"

Milla tugged on her hand, but it would not

budge. There was magic at work here, magic that worked through the water her hand had touched.

For a moment Milla considered cutting off her hand. But that would reduce her chances of surviving long enough to return to the Ruin Ship and deliver the Sunstone. It might have to be done, but she should try everything else first.

Milla looked up, but Odris had come no closer. Either the Storm Shepherd was biding her time before coming to help, or she was sulking over Milla's behaviour towards her.

"I am Milla." She didn't bother announcing her parentage. It would mean nothing to this strange water spirit. "What do you want of me?"

"Ah, she speaks," said the Face, and the whole lake tilted up so it could look at her. "I want nothing, save a little conversation to pass the idle days. It is lonely here and I am forbidden to slosh my way to more interesting parts."

"I do not like talk," said Milla. "Let me go."

The Face smiled, its watery lips curving back.

"No, no," it said. "It is not as simple as that.

I am bound here and must play my part. You have come here and must play yours."

"What part?" asked Milla. "I am no singer, to imitate the voices of others."

"You wear a Sunstone," said the Face. "And I see you have a Storm Shepherd. It is destined to be your new Spiritshadow, I would guess, and you a Chosen who has recently bound it. Congratulations."

"I am not a Chosen," Milla said, but her words were smothered by a crash of thunder from overhead as lightning flashed down into the water.

"You are aided by an angry Storm Shepherd," said the Face, smiling again. "But lightning can do nothing to a lake. Though it *could* do much to a Chosen." A trickle of water shot out from where the face's chin would be and circled around Milla's foot.

Milla tried to lift her foot, but the water was like glue. She could only get her heel a few finger-widths off the ground before the water sucked it back down.

The Icecarl considered cutting at the water, but that was almost certain not to work and would only make her look foolish. Once again she regretted not knowing how to use her Sunstone. A proper blast from that could boil the lake like Selski blubber in a melting pot. She didn't think the Face would enjoy being turned into steam.

But she didn't know how to blast it. And she couldn't fight it. It was a very strange feeling. There was nothing on the Dark World she couldn't at least try to fight.

"What do you want?" she asked again.

9

"A game," said the Face. "We will play a riddle game. If you can answer three riddles, I will let you go. I will even give you a gift. For each riddle you cannot answer you will stay with me for a hundred days and we will talk. As I said, it is lonely here. Too many travellers know of my fondness for conversation."

Riddling was popular among Icecarls, but Milla had never been good at it, or particularly interested. Riddling was Crone-work really, or for singers and Sword-Thanes.

"Don't I get to ask *you* three riddles?" she asked. She could not possibly let herself be trapped here for even one day, let alone a hundred.

"No," replied the Face. It pouted its great watery lips. "It is my game, not yours."

"Can I ask Odris – the Storm Shepherd – to answer with me?" asked Milla.

"For one riddle," said the Face, after a moment's thought. "Are you ready?"

Milla nodded.

"Here is riddle the first," said the Face.

"A maiden's head so deathly still
Cold and quiet, yet not ill
Her long tresses hang towards the sky
Hair that burns when it is dry
Food to man and creature's lair
Name both her and her hair."

Milla listened without expression, committing the words to memory. Odris drifted down towards her.

"I know," the Storm Shepherd said eagerly. "It's—"

"Quiet," ordered Milla. She didn't want to waste the Storm Shepherd's help so early. If the Face asked her a riddle that depended on some knowledge of Aenir, she would have to rely on Odris, much as she hated to do so.

"But I know!" exclaimed Odris. "Why are you so difficult? I wish I'd picked the other one."

Milla ignored her. She was going over all the riddles she knew in case they inspired her. The answers to most of the Icecarls' riddles could be found in their everyday lives. That might be the case here. But what would the everyday life of this strange Face in the water be like? There was nothing here except the lake and whatever was in it...

In it. That was the clue. Milla laughed as she looked into the water. It had been staring her in the face all the time.

"She is a rock," said the Icecarl. "Her hair is the seaweed that grows from the rock."

"Too easy, too easy," groaned the Face. "I must find something more difficult. A tricky riddle for a smart Chosen, yes?"

"No," said Milla. "I am not—"

Once again thunder smothered her words, but the lightning struck the earth on the far side of the lake. Whatever Odris was playing at she was being careful. Milla frowned as she also recognised that she now knew much more about lightning than she ever had before. Like the fact that if a bolt hit water near her, its force could travel through the water and hurt her. No one had told Milla about this. She just knew it.

It had to be a result of her shadow being absorbed by the Storm Shepherd.

"I have it!" said the Face. "This is riddle the second."

> "A traveller begins a journey. For the first week he is carried south. For the second week he carries others. In the third week he flies up into the sky. In the fourth week he falls back down. Who is the traveller?"

"That's it?" asked Odris incredulously. "That's the best you can do?"

"Quiet," ordered Milla again. She was annoyed that the Storm Shepherd seemed to know the answer already. Surely she could do better than a cloud-woman.

"This is a very hard riddle for a Chosen," chuckled the Face. "You'll never get this. We shall talk and talk and talk—"

"The traveller is an iceberg to begin with," interrupted Milla. "Then it is free-flowing water. Then it is water-cloud, as from a kettle or where the hot metal boils under the Ice. Then it is rain, or snow."

"That's not it!" groaned Odris.

"Yes it is," said the Face angrily. "You are no Chosen! No Chosen knows anything of icebergs. What are you?"

"I am an Icecarl," said Milla. "I am Milla of the Far Raiders. Daughter of Ylse, daughter of Emor, daughter of Rohen, daughter of Clyo, in the line of Danir since the Ruin of the Ship."

"Danir?" said the Face, its mouth and forehead twisted in rage. "Danir? You are of Danir's get!"

The whole Face reared up out of the water. Long teeth grew where none had been before and a great tongue came lashing out to grip Milla.

But before it could grab hold the Face suddenly froze. Ice crystals formed in a great ring around it and started to spread inwards in thousands of tiny branching lines.

The Face screamed and groaned and then settled back into the lake bed. The ice retreated and was soon gone.

Milla stood, still trapped, her heart hammering. She had been helpless, certain that she would be eaten – or perhaps drowned – by the Face. Then the ice had come. But from where?

"The riddle game binds you as much as Milla and must be played out to the end," said Odris to the Face. "But tell me. Who was Danir that you hate her so?"

"I will ask my third riddle," said the Face sullenly, ignoring Odris's question.

"Danir is the ancestor of my line," Milla answered. "I too am curious why she should have an enemy from another world, from a time so long ago."

"This is riddle the third," muttered the Face, ignoring them.

"There was a being proud and free, who
through no fault of its own was caught

up in a war between the rulers of two worlds. The war had gone on for many, many years and there was much hate between the two sides. Finally the war ended in a great working of magic. An arcane barrier was raised on one world to keep light – and the enemy – without. On the other world a spell caused most of the inhabitants to forget their powers and much of their past. Bereft of both memory and magic these once-proud beings were easily bound, each to its own allotted cell. Only a descendant of the original binder could free them, either by moving their binding from the place to their person or simply loosing their chains.

I am such a prisoner and I was bound here by Danir, who you claim as your far ancestress. Will you free me?"

"That's not a riddle," said Odris indignantly. "That's a question. Or a statement. Or something."

Milla frowned. It wasn't a riddle, but the Face seemed to sincerely believe that Milla could free it.

"I don't understand," she said. "Danir is the far ancestor of my clan, but she was an Icecarl. Icecarls have never come to this world, to Aenir. We live on the Ice, in the Dark World."

"I don't care what your people call you now," said the Face. "And I can't remember what you called yourselves then. All I know is that soon after the creation of the Veil and the Forgetting, I was bound here by a sorceress called Danir."

Milla shook her head. This was a matter for Crones to ponder over, not for a warrior. She longed for the clean Ice and an enemy that she could fight and kill. Not these games of words and magic.

"Even if the Danir who bound you was the same as my far ancestor, I do not have the knowledge to free you," Milla said. "I do not count this answer as the third in the game. You must ask a proper riddle."

"No, no," sobbed the Face, tears of darker water streaming down its cheeks. "You must free me. So many Chosen have come over the centuries, but none could free me, for none were of Danir's line. I would serve as your Spiritshadow—"

"She's already got me!" interrupted Odris. "What would she need a great lump of wet for?"

"Please," begged the Face. "I have sat here too long. Set me free!"

"I do not know how," whispered Milla. She felt the Face's desire for freedom. The worst punishment an Icecarl could imagine would be to be penned up and unable to move. If the Icecarls could not follow the Selski migration they would die.

"I do," said Odris. "Do you want me to tell you how?"

10

After a few hours of steady walking Tal had left the grasslands behind. Possibly they had been moving the other way as well, all the time. In Aenir it was hard to be sure.

The grass ended in a completely straight border that stretched as far as Tal could see to the north and south. On the western side it was grass, on the eastern a strange desert of red sand and spiky blue crystals that grew up in columns, looking from a distance almost like trees.

The major difference was that the crystals were very sharp and they seemed to be carnivorous. At least there were scraps of flesh and skin hanging off many of the "plants" and all of them were surrounded by rings of broken bones.

Tal gave each crystal plant a wide berth. As far as he could tell they couldn't move, but he didn't trust them. They might be like the trees of the forest where he'd arrived and would move when it suited them.

As he walked further into the desert it got much hotter. The crystals shone more brightly, with a hypnotic glare. This was how they caught their prey and Tal had to stop himself several times from walking into one of the plants. He wished for his old shadowguard. It would have shaded his head from the sun and shielded his eyes. But the shadowguard was gone, back to living its life as a growing Dattu.

Then Tal remembered that he did have a companion that could shade him. He stopped and looked up. Adras had been trailing behind quite high up. Now he was nowhere to be seen. But he wasn't too far away. Tal could feel his presence, a connection between them. He recognised it as being like the link he'd had with his shadowguard.

"Adras!" Tal shouted. His voice was hoarse. He'd drunk from a small stream that morning, but had been wanting another drink for some hours. This desert was much hotter than it had any right to be.

Adras did not answer his call.

Tal called again and listened. There was a faint boom up ahead, a rather pathetic thunderclap.

Tal sighed and began to slog towards the sound, carefully winding his way between the crystal plants.

A few hundred stretches further on he came to an oasis in the blue crystal desert – a patch of more usual earth with a small bubbling spring surrounded by a stand of tall, thin trees with greeny-purple fronds.

Adras was hovering above the spring, sucking up moisture. A thick column of vapour spun out of the spring and into his open mouth.

Tal hurried down to get a drink. There might be something to eat too, for the trees had fruit between the fronds.

There was also fruit on the ground. Tal had a drink then picked up a piece of fruit and examined it. It had a hard skin, but was soft and pulpy inside. He had seen such fruit before, though only in baskets brought to the Chosen Enclave. His mother had called it cakefruit, cut it into slices and cooked it in the oven.

Tal couldn't do that here, but he did roast the fruit with a beam of hot white light from his Sunstone until the pulp browned. Eating it brought back memories of better times when his family was all together and the worst thing Tal had to worry about was going back to a new term at the Lectorium.

Tal spat out the last mouthful of cakefruit. He didn't want to remember any more. It was too dispiriting to think about his family and their troubles. He had to focus on the immediate objective.

"I have to find the Codex," he said aloud.

Above him Adras nodded his head, but did not stop soaking up water vapour. The desert had been hard on the Storm Shepherd. He had shrunk to three quarters his normal size in the dry air. Now he was intent on taking in as much water as possible to last him until the cooler night.

"It's better that Milla left," Tal added. He was looking at Adras, but he was really talking to himself. "It makes everything more... I don't know... straightforward. I mean, she didn't want to find the Codex really. She just wanted to know about Aenir to tell that weird old woman."

Adras stopped taking in water vapour long enough to burp. Then he started sucking again, his powerful breath twisting the water into vapour and up into his mouth.

"Beautiful," said Tal. "You're a big help."

Despite the heat, now at its most intense, Tal didn't want to wait. Every minute spent in the oasis was time lost. Anything could be happening while he sat around eating cakefruit. To Gref, or to his mother.

Anything.

"Come on," he said. But he had only gone a few stretches from the shade of the trees when the heat from the sand burnt through the soles of his shoes, sending him hopping and swearing back to the pool.

"Too hot to travel," said Adras, yawning. "We should wait till it cools off."

"I guess so," said Tal reluctantly. He inspected his boots. He hadn't noticed before, but the morning's trek through the strange desert had burned several holes through the hide. They were Icecarl boots, built for ice, not burning sands. "We'll have to make up the time tonight."

Adras nodded.

Tal put his back against one of the trees, looked up to make sure that no cakefruit was likely to fall on him and closed his eyes. He wouldn't sleep, he vowed. He'd just think everything through. Finding the Codex was the first step, but there was a lot more to think about.

"How do I find the Codex?" he mumbled to himself. Did he just keep on walking east till he fell over it?

Tal knew it wouldn't be as easy as that. He would rest now and save his strength. Then he would walk all night. He'd make up the lost time. He had to.

But the sun was very hot, even in the shade of the cakefruit trees, and Tal's thoughts drifted off into dreams.

He slept, even when the breeze came up and cakefruit dropped with soft plopping noises all around him.

He slept on, even as something slithered down

the trunk of the cakefruit tree above him. Something long and scaly, though very flat and thin. It had thousands of tiny hooked legs. They rippled under it, each hook digging out minute flecks of bark as it made its circular way down and round the trunk.

It had two heads at the end of its ribbonlike body. They were of unequal sizes. The smaller head had a bulbous cluster of eight multifaceted eyes and two jointed tendrils that quested ahead. The other head was twice as big. It was all mouth, currently shut.

The thing seemed in no hurry. It moved steadily down until it was right above Tal's sleeping head. The tendrils from its small head brushed his hair and the eyes glittered as it measured up the Chosen boy.

Then its mouth began to open. At first it didn't seem possible that it could open wide enough to do Tal any harm. But the lower section of the thing's head continued to open wider and wider, the mouth spreading back well past the second head and into the creature's body.

It didn't have any teeth, but an ugly green spit began to drip from the back of its throat.

The thing shifted a little to line Tal up better and then slowly began to lower its jaws down over his head, as the green drool spread across his scalp.

11

Tal awoke to the sound of strange rumbling and a sun that was low in the sky. He sat up a little straighter and scratched his head. Something sticky came off on his hand and Tal jerked his fingers back down to look.

"Errrch!" he yelled, and stood up. Some disgusting tree sap or something had dropped on his head while he was asleep. He rushed over to the spring and washed his hand off, then stuck his head in and gave that a good wash as well.

The level of the spring had sunk a good hand's breadth and it was easy to see where it had gone as well as where the strange rumbling sound was coming from. Adras was floating just above Tal's head, snoring. He had taken in so much water he was a fat butterball of a cloud, all fluffy white, without a streak of the lean, mean darkness of a storm.

"Call yourself a Storm Shepherd!" said Tal, but he didn't say it too loud. He could hardly blame Adras for falling asleep. He was disgusted that he had himself, though they probably would not have been able to set out any earlier anyway.

Mind you, he thought, it was lucky nothing happened. Aenir was not a world where it paid to sleep unguarded.

He was just thinking that when he saw the hideous creature with two heads. It was on the ground only a few stretches away wriggling towards him, a trail of the hideous green slime dribbling from its mouth.

Tal raised his hand and focused on the Sunstone. He would blast it with a Red Ray of Fiery Destruction.

The Sunstone flashed red and began to shine. But before the Red Ray was complete, Tal blinked and lowered his hand.

The grotesque two-headed worm or snake, or whatever it was, had left a trail of its own bright saliva in particular patterns. It had scribed a whole series of characters on to the ground under the trees.

Tal stared at the writing. At first he couldn't work it out. Then he realised that he was looking at everything upside down. So he walked round, taking care to give plenty of space to the two-headed snake, which was still writing.

There was the letter C again and an arrow pointing east. But there was also a picture of something. A key, Tal thought. And then several letters which spelled out H-A-Z-R-O-R.

"Who are you?" asked Tal, talking to the snake. "How do you communicate through creatures?"

The snake twitched and began to drip another letter on to the ground. Tal walked a bit closer, keen to work out what the letter was going to be. It looked like the first part of a C.

He was only a stretch away when there was a titanic explosion of air. Tal was thrown backwards and a great spray of dirt shot into the sky, accompanied by pieces of two-headed snake.

"I got it!" roared Adras, punching the air with one huge cloud-fist. "I've saved you!"

Tal picked himself up and counted to ten. Adras was worse than Gref. At least Gref *knew* he was annoying when he interfered with whatever Tal was doing.

"Why did you do that?" Tal asked slowly, when he could get the words out without screaming.

"It was a Two-Headed Gulper," said Adras, as if that was explanation enough. "Lucky I was keeping an eye open."

This was too much for Tal.

"You were sound asleep, you idiot!" he shouted. "And it was writing me a message. A message from the Codex!"

"It wasn't a Two-Headed Gulper?" asked Adras innocently.

"Yes, it was," agreed Tal. "But it wasn't... I don't know... being one right at that second."

"What have you done to your hair?" asked Adras, tilting his puffy head to one side as if he couldn't work it out.

"What?" asked Tal. "What?"

"Your hair," said Adras. "It's changed colour."

Tal forgot about telling the Storm Shepherd exactly how stupid he was and rushed over to the spring. But it was bubbling too much to be a useful mirror.

"Green," added Adras. "In streaks."

Tal touched his hair again. It seemed all right, but when he pulled out a few hairs they were bright green.

As green as the saliva of the Two-Headed Gulper he realised. It must have been dripping on his head, just before it was taken over – or whatever the Codex did – and made to write the message.

He looked back at the tree where he'd been sleeping and saw the pattern of the Gulper's clawed feet heading down and a few patches of green on the bark just above where his head would have been.

"I feel sick," he said suddenly.

Adras watched in total puzzlement as the boy staggered over to another tree and threw up. It seemed rather an excessive reaction just because his hair had changed colour. Storm Shepherds changed colour all the time.

When Tal had stopped being sick he turned back to Adras.

"Adras," said Tal. "I think it's time we set down some rules. First of all, you must not go to sleep when I am asleep. You must keep watch."

"But I feel sleepy when you're sleepy," answered Adras. "Because we share a bond."

"I am the Chosen," ordered Tal. "You are my Spiritshadow. Or you will be. You must obey."

"Why?" asked Adras. "Why shouldn't we work things out together?"

Tal stared up at the sky. This was not how he'd imagined dealing with his own Spiritshadow. If only Milla hadn't interrupted him back at the Hill, he would have bound this hulking great creature properly. Now Tal had given away his shadow, instead of using it to secure absolute obedience.

Adras mistook Tal's silence for some sort of sulk.

"Well, if that's the way you want it," he said, "I'll sleep when you're awake. I'll sleep now."

"No!" exclaimed Tal. "We need to keep moving.

The sky is clear – I'll be able to see well enough to find a path through the crystals."

"But where?" asked Adras. "To find Odris?"

"No!" said Tal. "We've been over that. The Codex – at least I think it's the Codex – has sent me another message."

He frowned, thinking about the arrow and the pictures of the key and the letters that spelled out "Hazror".

"We will head east and there is somewhere called Hazror, where we will look for a key," Tal announced confidently. It was important to sound in charge in front of a wayward servant. He'd learned that as a child, instructing Underfolk.

He didn't feel confident though. What if he'd got the message totally wrong?

"Hazror?" asked Adras. "Haze-roar?"

"Yes," said Tal. "Do you know anything about it?"

"I know something about a *creature* called Hazror," said Adras. His chest turned dark and stormy and lightning flashed at his fingertips. "Enough to know that we don't want to go anywhere *near* him."

12

"No," said Milla, after she considered what Odris had said, and the Face's plea for freedom. "If Danir did indeed bind you here, it is not for me to free you."

The Face snarled at this answer. Only the spell that bound it in place and the pact of the riddle game prevented it from attacking Milla.

"But I will report what you have told me to the Crones," Milla added. "I do not think Danir would want any living thing fixed in one place for so long."

"Tell the Crones!" spat the Face, a spray of cold water splashing over Milla. "What use is that to me?"

"It may be, one day," said Milla calmly. "Now you must release me. I have answered three riddles."

"The third was not a riddle," grumbled the Face. "I will ask another. Riddle the—"

It stopped, its tongue suddenly frosted, frozen in place. Its eyes rolled and its cheeks swelled as it tried to continue speaking, but the frost held it fast.

Milla looked down and saw that the thin trickle of water that held her foot was frozen. Experimentally she tried to shift her leg. The ice cracked and broke.

She tried to move her hand. The water droplets there were now flecks of ice and they fell off.

She was free!

She ran around the pool and away. Odris cruised above her calling back towards the Face.

"Hah! That's what you get when you try and cheat on the riddle game!" the Storm Shepherd shouted.

Milla and Odris were a hundred stretches away when the Face's tongue unfroze. They heard its shout behind them, plaintive and sad.

"Remember! Speak to your Crones! Free me!"

They heard the Face calling for almost an hour after that, its voice fading as the distance between them slowly increased.

The grassland gave way to a sparse forest of grey, sick-looking trees. After examining them carefully to make sure they were not likely to move or attack her, Milla cut several branches and sharpened the ends into points to create makeshift spears. They did not throw well, but they were serviceable. She also picked up several smooth stones, again checking them carefully to make sure they were not eggs or something worse.

Odris watched from overhead without comment. Milla was tempted to ask the Storm Shepherd about the trees and the stones, but she chose not to. She must not become dependent on the creature, the Icecarl told herself.

Milla walked through the forest for several hours. After a while the ground started to rise. It was quite gradual, but even so it placed an extra strain on her bruised ankles and knees. So she told Odris to pick her up again, to fly for a while.

"I'm too tired," said Odris. "Besides, why should I carry you? You haven't been nice to me at all."

"I didn't ask you to eat my shadow," said Milla. "Give it back and I will go on alone."

"I didn't *eat* it. I'm sharing it. And I can't give it back."

"Tell me. What was the Face talking about back there? What war between two worlds?"

"Will you be nice to me if I tell you?"

"Shield Maidens do not barter favours." Milla started walking again.

"Oh, all right, I'll tell you anyway," said Odris. "The war was between the world you come from and Aenir. I don't know much about it really, because I'm only two thousand years old and it happened just before I was created. Nearly every Aeniran who was alive back then suffered the Forgetting, so they couldn't tell me what happened either. I've just picked up pieces of the story here and there."

Two thousand years, thought Milla. A year was a circling, she knew, or close enough. She silently counted through the generations back to Danir. It did add up. Danir would have been living roughly two thousand years ago. But she was an Icecarl ancestor, not one of the Chosen.

"The Face spoke of the Veil being made at the

same time as the Forgetting," said Milla. She'd stopped walking, intent on the questions she was asking. "Who made the Veil? And who... how... was the Forgetting done?"

"I'm not really sure," replied Odris. Her lightning-eyes were very bright – she was clearly interested in this subject. "The people on your world – the ones that now call themselves the Chosen, though they had a different name then – made the Veil to keep Aeniran creatures out of your world. Because we have always become shadows in your world, blocking the sun was the ultimate defence. However the Veil was only part of the plan, which was carried out by two different sorts of Chosen. The first kind created the Veil. The second kind cast the Forgetting and bound almost every Aeniran in place while we were weak and powerless from the Forgetting. These Chosen bound everyone, whether we'd been shadows in your world or not. Danir was one of this second sort of Chosen, I'm sure."

"But what happened to them?" asked Milla. "The ones who did the Forgetting and the Binding?"

"When the job was done they left Aenir and went back to your world," said Odris. "For a long time after that everyone on Aenir was stuck within their bounds. You know, in a cave, or on a hill, or in a lake or whatever. It was very boring. Then the Chosen showed up again and released lots of us to be Spiritshadows. They took young Aenirans to be shadowguards and quite a few Aenirans got released by accident as well. Only no one wanted to bind Adras and me as Spiritshadows until you and your friend Tal came along—"

"He is not my friend!" Milla said. She started walking again. There was much to think about. She had always known that there was a time before the Veil, but not that the barrier against the sun had been created to keep out Aenirans. Though it made sense. They became shadows on her world, and would be greatly weakened by darkness.

The Forgetting and the Binding of the Aenirans was also very interesting. It sounded like exactly the sort of thing that the Crones could do, which suggested that "the second sort of Chosen" were in fact Icecarls.

It all added up to the horrible realisation that two thousand years ago Chosen and Icecarls had joined together to fight against the threat from Aenir. Then they had gone about their separate ways. But now the Chosen seemed to be undoing everything that had been won. They were releasing Aenirans and taking them to the Dark World to become Spiritshadows. And their excessive use of Sunstones weakened the defence against Spiritshadows offered by the Veil.

Milla wondered if the Crones knew about all this. Did they know about Aenir, and the War, and their ancestors' part in it? Did they know what the Chosen were doing to Aenirans and what it could mean to the Icecarls?

Something moved ahead of Milla, interrupting her thoughts. Whatever it was it was coming straight towards her. Without thinking she threw the stone in her hand. It whizzed between the trees and struck with a loud and fatal-sounding crack.

13

Milla drew her sword and advanced cautiously.

A small fluffy creature lay on the ground, its head crushed by the stone. Milla prodded it cautiously with her sword. It had the same sort of strange, thin fur on light bones that she'd seen before on the singing animals in the trees. Birds, as Tal had called them. But this bird had no wings and it had been running along the ground. And it was blue all over except for its pointy beak, which was bright red.

"What is this called?" Milla asked Odris.

"Nanuch," said Odris. "Stupid and single-minded. They come in—"

Before she could finish several more birds came running straight at Milla. The leader leaped up at her face and struck savagely with its pointed beak. Milla ducked and struck back, but it had already run on, not looking back. She barely had time to turn as three more jumped up at her. Milla got the first one with a flung stone and then quickly stabbed the other two. But there were even more behind them all running in a single, straight line straight towards her.

"Flocks," continued Odris. "They should ignore you if you get out of the way. There's something else about them too, but I can't remember..."

Milla kicked the dead birds aside and got out of the way. She stood watching in disbelief for a long time after that as a seemingly inexhaustible line of stupid bright blue birds ran past.

If she'd known they wanted right of way she'd have given it to them.

When the last bird had passed, Milla picked up the dead ones. They looked like they'd make good eating, if she could cook them.

She'd just thrust the last one's head through her

belt and made sure it wouldn't fall out when Odris swooped down and held out her hands.

"Time to go up!"

Milla was about to ask why when she saw a much, much larger version of the same blue, red-beaked bird she'd just put in her belt come crashing through the trees.

A giant Nanuch.

It was followed by three more, but they weren't running stupidly in line. They were weaving their way carefully around the trees and their fierce and intelligent eyes were looking everywhere about them.

The lead bird saw Milla and the carcasses arrayed round her belt.

It clacked its beak, a sharp, urgent sound that was louder than a shout. It was immediately echoed by all the other birds Milla could see – and even more of them somewhere behind.

Milla didn't wait to count them. These birds were as tall as she was, their beaks were as long as her sword and she could hear them clacking all over the place.

She held up her arms in one swift motion. Odris gripped them.

"Unnnhh," grunted the Storm Shepherd as she took off straight up. Milla pulled up her legs as far as they could go just as the lead bird leaped at her. Its sharp beak stabbed empty air a hairbreadth under her feet.

Odris grunted again and stopped rising.

"Up! Up!" shouted Milla. She wished she'd kept one hand free now to fight back. But it was too late. Odris had her in a grip that could not be broken.

"I'm trying!" shouted Odris.

The bird jumped up at Milla again and this time its beak slashed across the sole of her boot. It didn't get through, but Milla felt it. Its beak was sharp.

"You're too heavy!" said Odris, though she did rise up a little.

"Let go of my left arm," ordered Milla quickly. There were three birds below her now, all jumping up to attack. A slightly smarter one was backing up the hill to take a running leap.

Odris let go of her arm and Milla quickly pulled one of the dead birds out of her belt. She swung it round and round and then let it fly off into the distance.

As she'd hoped, two of the big birds chased after it including the one who'd backed up the hill.

She repeated the process with all the dead birds and all were chased. But there were so many more huge Nanuch arriving that it didn't make much difference.

It did lighten the load a bit, so Odris was able to go higher. She also started to glide away, with the birds following underneath. Their beak-clacking was so loud that it sounded like a hailstorm.

Milla would have preferred that. She knew how to survive a hailstorm.

"I'm not sure how long I can keep you up!" puffed Odris after they had travelled a few hundred stretches with the birds still trailing along underneath.

"Keep going!" Milla encouraged the Storm Shepherd. She could see some of the big birds turning back, obviously to go after the single file of the lesser birds. Their children, she thought. Or maybe their parents. Who knew on this strange world?

"I really can't keep going," Odris panted. "I need water."

"Just a bit further," urged Milla. The crowd of birds chasing them was thinning out. "Can't you hit a few with your lightning?"

"Not unless you want to get hit too," panted Odris. She dropped a stretch and several birds leaped up, beaks flashing in the sun. They only missed Milla because she swung herself violently up her feet striking Odris under her armpit.

"Whoa!" exclaimed the Storm Shepherd. She shot up several stretches, well out of the bird's reach.

Milla didn't reply, though she noted that Odris had greater strength than she was admitting to. That was an enemy's trick, not one you expected from an ally.

"Ah, look there!" exclaimed Odris. She swung her arm forwards to point, forgetting that Milla was attached and they both went into a spin that took them dangerously close to the birds again.

For a moment all Milla saw were red beaks and blue feathers then Odris managed to right herself and the Icecarl saw what the Storm Shepherd had been pointing at.

There was a building ahead. A strange building.

It was a tower that had been carved out of the stump of a truly mighty tree, a vast block of grey and green, with stunted branches cut clean close to the trunk. The stump was at least as tall as the mast of the Far Raiders' iceship, and forty stretches in diameter. It had many narrow windows, but there was no sign of a door or gate on the side Milla could see.

But better than that, it had a flat walkway around its crown. If Odris could get high enough she could land Milla there.

"The top!" shouted Milla. "Take me to the top!"

"I can't!" shrieked Odris. "I'm falling!"

Below them, the Nanuch jumped, clacking their beaks even louder as it looked like their enemy might escape.

14

It turned out that Adras didn't really know anything about Hazror, except that it wasnt the name of a place, but of a creature. A very bad and truly terrible creature.

Like the grassland before it the desert of blue crystal trees ended suddenly. The border was once again an exact straight line. On the other side there was soft yellow sand, piling up into dunes as far as Tal could see.

Tal walked over and his feet sank in halfway to his ankles. The sand was still very hot, even though the sun was setting and it was long past the full heat of the day.

Wearily Tal picked a dune that looked to be east from its opposition to the setting sun and started to trudge.

He had gone up and down two dunes and was resting at the top of the third, wondering whether to try and camp there for the night, when he saw something flash further along the ridge of sand.

It flashed again and he realised that it was coming towards him.

"Adras!" Tal called. "Watch out!"

"I'm watching," rumbled Adras. He'd lost some of the extra water he'd taken on. It had evaporated while crossing the blue crystal desert and now the hot sands, but he was still fat and rather slow to move.

Tal raised his Sunstone. He wouldn't be caught napping this time.

As it drew closer, Tal recognised the creature. It was a thin animal about the length of his forearm, with long, spindly legs and short forearms. It had a short tail and a long, thin snout. But its most distinctive characteristic was the silvery sheen of its skin. That skin was made up of many tiny, armoured scales, but they were not like a reptile's.

Under its armour the creature was a mammal. The females even had pouches to carry their young.

It was a Samheal Semidragon.

Tal knew of it from the Beastmaker game. But he couldn't remember whether they were aggressive. Samheal Semidragons were always played for Skin, not Temper or anything else.

He also wasn't sure if there was anything he could do to hurt it. That silver skin was protection against heat as well as weapons, though something sufficiently sharp wielded with enough strength would get through.

A two-handed axe in the hands of a Borzog might be enough. Unfortunately all Tal had was his Sunstone. And Adras.

He hoped that Samheal Semidragons were friendly.

This one stopped a few paces away, skidding to a halt on its back legs. It stood upright and waved its paws at Tal, making skittering noises.

"Tch-tch-tch," it said.

Tal shook his head.

"Adras. Do you know what it said?"

"Tch-tch-tch," repeated Adras. "Whatever that means."

"Thanks," said Tal. He should have known better than to ask.

The Semidragon hopped forwards and swept the dune clean behind it with its tail. Then it turned round and with one silver claw began to trace a line in the sand.

"The Codex!" exclaimed Tal. "I wonder if this is another messenger?"

He felt fairly sure it was the Codex using these animals somehow, a confidence reinforced when the Semidragon looked back at him and traced out the letter C. After that it drew another arrow, pointing east across the sand. Then it drew a key again, but this time it also drew another picture next to it. Something that looked like a pipe or a tube with several holes drilled into it.

"What's that?" asked Tal.

The Semidragon didn't answer. It stared around in fright, as if it had suddenly found itself aware of its surroundings. Its muscles tensed to jump away. Before it could, a shudder went through its small body. Its eyes clouded and it settled down. A moment later it drew another symbol.

Tal stared down at the rough mark. It was a musical note, written in the notation the Chosen used to perform in the Crystal Wood, back in the Castle. But what did it mean, a single note all by itself? It was a very high one, too high for Tal or any human to sing or hum. It could only be created by light of the correct colour striking the right crystal in the Wood.

The Semidragon started to draw something else, but it stopped in mid-motion and shuddered again. This time it did jump away, leaving the last letter or picture unfinished.

It looked like an unfinished drawing of a human skull, Tal thought, but it was probably meant to be part of a letter. He wished that the Semidragon had been able to finish it. Obviously the Codex could only use such animals briefly. Still, it had given him some more information.

If only he knew what it meant.

He kept thinking about it all as he trudged on, but his thoughts were beginning to wander in the direction of food and shelter for the night. Neither looked likely to appear in this sandy desert.

Yet over the next sand dune, as the last light faded from the sky, Tal did see something that might offer shelter of some kind. A few ruined walls jutted out of the sand in the hollow below him. Just four corners, with nothing between them and no roof overhead. But it would be better than trying to sleep on top of a sand dune.

He started down. Adras followed above and behind, muttering something to himself. Tal didn't even try to listen.

Closer to the ruins it became clear that the building had not been a normal house. There were too many stones lying around it, scattered through the sand. It must have been a fortification of some kind, Tal realised. Or else there were a lot of other foundations nearby buried under the sand.

There was also something painted on one of the walls. A sign of some kind. Two rough circles, one inside the other. In the twilight it was hard to see what they were painted with, but Tal had a nasty suspicion it was blood.

He had never seen the sign before and did not know what it meant.

But Adras did. The Storm Shepherd stopped abruptly and rumbled, "Beware! This is Hazror's place."

"What?" asked Tal. "This ruin?"

"Yes," said a voice that was soft and strangely childlike. It issued out of the ground seemingly from several places at once.

The sand in front of Tal suddenly started to shift sideways, as if moved by a giant invisible hand. In a few seconds, it had cleared away to reveal stone steps going down. A long way down.

"Come in," said the voice. It sounded strangely familiar to Tal though not in a reassuring way. Like the voice of someone he knew, but disturbingly altered.

He peered down at the newly revealed steps. The sand was being held back by walls of light, very similar to the ones that Ebbitt had used to hold back the water when he'd helped Tal escape from the Pit back in the Castle.

Tal looked at the light walls very carefully,

noting the flecks of colour. It was mostly Yellow but occasionally Blue. Whoever was making these walls appear had a powerful Sunstone and was very good at using it.

Better than Ebbitt, because there was no sand leaking through these walls.

Hazror must be a Chosen.

If the walls collapsed while Tal was down there, he would have no way out. Unless he could move the sand back himself.

Tal considered that prospect. He thought he could build himself a tunnel of light through the sand. If he had to.

He took a step forwards on to the steps.

"Don't go!" Adras pleaded. He wrung his hands together and a couple of buckets of rain fell down, narrowly missing Tal. "Hazror will eat you. Then I will be eaten too."

"Don't be ridiculous," said Tal, though he said it with more confidence than he felt. He indicated the walls of light that lined the steps. "Hazror has to be a Chosen. We don't eat people. Besides, I don't have a choice. I *have* to find the Codex."

He started down the steps. Then he looked back and said, "Stay there until I come back."

He looked back again when he was halfway down and saw the walls of light close in behind him. Sand poured back down.

On the surface there was no sign of the stairs or of Tal. There were only sand, ruins and a cloud that spun round in a circle crying, "I told you not to go!"

21

Odris was falling. Or she was until Milla swung up and fluttered her hand across Odris's armpit.

"Ah!" screeched the Storm Shepherd. She suddenly climbed even higher than the stump tower ahead. "Stop! Eee! Ah! It tickles!"

Milla didn't stop tickling. Odris shivered and shook from side to side but she also kept climbing. The Nanuch were left far below, jumping and clacking their beaks in disappointment.

"Stop! Stop!" giggled Odris. "I can't stand it!"

"I'll stop when you put me down on top of the tower," said Milla grimly. She was disappointed in the Storm Shepherd. Odris clearly had plenty of strength left if a mere tickling could produce this surge of energy.

Giggling and shaking, Odris complied. She dropped Milla on the walkway and then collapsed herself, a thick layer of fog draped round the spire.

Milla had half expected to see some guard or watchman on the walkway, hidden behind the central spire. But there was no one there. She walked around and saw an open door and a circular stairway, but the tower was quiet and there was no hint of anyone coming up.

Closer it was hard to work out how the tower had been made. It *was* carved out of a gigantic stump. But there were no signs of tools upon the wood. No chisel marks or any other evidence that people had done the work.

Milla couldn't even begin to imagine how big the original tree must have been. Ten or twelve times the height of the Ruin Ship at least. As tall as a small mountain.

Another oddity was the faint smell of burning, as if there had been a recent fire. But there was no sign of a fire upon the wood. All Milla could see was the natural grain and the thousands and thousands of growth rings spreading in circles under her feet.

"You shouldn't have tickled me," said Odris reproachfully.

"You shouldn't have lied about your strength," said Milla. "Come on. I'm going downstairs."

"I need a rest," said Odris. "I'll wait here."

"Do what you will," said Milla. She went through the door and disappeared.

After a moment Odris sighed and wafted over to the door. She put her head in and then forced her shoulders through, her cloud-body ballooning up behind her. Gradually her body reshaped itself till she was longer and thinner, and the rest of her followed her head and arms down the stairway.

An hour later Odris came squirming back the same way, followed by Milla. They had visited every level of the strange tower but had found nothing of interest. Every room was empty. Stranger still, there was a door at the bottom. An open door, which the Nanuch had made no attempt to enter. There were still twenty or thirty of them hanging around, but they simply watched Milla when she stood looking out through the doorway.

This disturbed the Icecarl. There had to be some reason that the giant birds were afraid to enter the tower. Perhaps it was the lair of some awful creature that would soon return. Or perhaps it was the smell of burnt wood. It was stronger on the lower levels, but there were still no signs of fire damage.

The rooftop was the safest place Milla decided, which was why they had climbed back up. If some creature did return to the tower they would hear it coming up the stairs. And it kept them out of reach of the waiting Nanuch. It looked like a dedicated score of the giant birds were determined to wait her out. She could see them clustered around the tower.

Even so Milla was uneasy. The tower was too good a shelter to be so deserted. On her world there would be all sorts of animals and insects living in it, taking cover from the elements.

But the tower was completely devoid of life. She hadn't even seen a caveroach or a spider.

"We'll stay here till dawn," she said to Odris finally. "Then we will see if the Nanuch still wait. You may have to carry me again."

"I'm not sure I can," said Odris. "I think I've lost too much water vapour. I need to build up. You must be thirsty too."

Milla didn't answer. She was thirsty, and hungry. But she had practised suppressing hunger pangs and water cravings almost all her life. It was a pity she had been forced to throw all the small Nanuch away. She could have eaten one raw, or tried once more to get heat from her Sunstone to cook it.

"I'll take the first watch," Milla announced. "You sleep."

Odris looked at the sun. It was still some way from setting.

"But I'm not sleepy," the Storm Shepherd said. "We don't usually sleep very much. It's only since I've been bound to you that I get sleepy."

"Then don't sleep," said Milla. "But be quiet."

Odris sniffed. She really did wish she'd picked the other one. It was typical of Adras. He wasn't smart, but he *was* lucky.

They sat in silence for a long time after that, listening to the sounds around them. The Nanuch settled down too, except for the occasional bout of beak-clacking. There were other, more distant noises – the calls of strange creatures. Once something flew past, too quick to be seen.

The sun set and the stars came out. Milla stretched and paced, her legs still sore from the Hugthing.

Hours passed, but when the time came for Odris to watch, Milla did not go to sleep. The more she paced upon the top of the tower, the more she felt like it was not a refuge but a trap.

Finally she decided they should try and sneak past the Nanuch before the dawn. Immediately she felt better. Taking action was the Shield Maiden way. She would never be one now, but at least she could act like one. And die like one if that was how it ended.

Once again they went down the stairs. Milla trod as lightly as she could and the only sound Odris made could be mistaken for the wind through the tower windows.

At the bottom Milla drew her dagger. Her sword's natural luminescence would alert the Nanuch.

Unfortunately there was no dust or dirt she could smear her furs or Selski-hide breastplate with, but at least the armour was fairly dark. She didn't put on her face mask. It was white bone and would shine too brightly under the stars. It felt strange going out to fight without it.

Milla crouched by the door for quite a long time, letting her eyes adjust to the starlit forest outside. It was bright enough to make out the shapes of trees – and several Nanuch. They stood completely still, never moving. Milla hoped this meant they were asleep.

She slid out through the door.

At least that's what she thought she did. But somehow she ended up back inside the lower room looking out.

Puzzled she stepped forwards again. For an instant she was in the doorway with her foot about to land on the bare earth outside.

Then it came down on a wooden floor. She had stepped through the door, but it didn't lead outside. It took her back inside.

There was some magic at work. Dire magic, Milla thought. Worse than anything she'd expected.

Now she was sure it was a trap.

16

Tal heard the slither of the sand pouring back behind him, but he didn't look around. The light walls on either side of him stayed steady and comforting. The stairs continued down in front.

They came to an end in front of a tall doorway. Obviously it had once been blocked by the enormous stone door that lay half across it, as if someone had ripped it open and let it fall.

That made Tal stop for a moment. But the Codex had told him to come here, he reasoned.

Finding the Codex meant finding Gref.

He who hesitates heads Redward, she who seizes opportunity soars to Violet.

Ebbitt used to repeat that back to front and laugh his head off, but Tal took the saying seriously.

He climbed over the fallen door and through the doorway.

The room beyond had walls of stone and light, both holding back sand, judging from the piles that had oozed through gaps where the magic barriers intersected with the stone.

In the middle of the room a boy sat cross-legged, staring at Tal. A boy not much older than Tal, dressed in white trousers and a white shirt with blue cuffs. A Chosen boy.

Tal even knew who it was: Lenan of the Blue. He had disappeared last year. Every Day of Ascension all the Chosen children who had come of age would go forth to seek a Spiritshadow to bind. Not all of them came back.

But what was Lenan doing here? And where was Hazror?

"Greetings, Chosen," said Lenan. His voice sounded a little strange. Too high-pitched.

Tal had started to walk forwards to greet Lenan properly, but when he heard the voice he stopped.

The voice wasn't the only thing that was strange. Lenan was wearing several Sunstones round his neck. One was bright, obviously working to keep the walls in place. But the boy had two more, both sparkling, though not currently active.

There was something odd about the light in the room as well. The walls were shifting through several colours, which was reasonable, as it made them stronger. But now that Tal looked at them, he realised that the overall colour in the room was a sickly grey. No normal Chosen ever used that colour.

Tal raised his hand and bright white flashed out, flooding every corner of the room.

In its stark illumination, Tal saw that Lenan was not really Lenan. The Chosen boy was just a picture woven from light, masking something much larger. An only approximately human thing of rotting flesh and naked bone that rose up and cast its disguise away.

This was what Adras was afraid of.

Hazror.

The three Sunstones Lenan had worn were not an illusion. Hazror picked one up in a hand that was more claw than anything else. Light flickered in the stone, building in intensity.

Tal didn't wait for whatever Hazror was going to do. In the first flash of white light he'd seen what he'd come for. Hanging around Hazror's neck, next to the Sunstones, was a thin tube. A tube with three holes.

Tal recognised it instantly. A whistle made of the same material as the trees in the Crystal Wood. It had to be what the Codex had told him to get.

He'd also seen the piles of bones around Hazror's feet and the broken skulls. They were human and most looked less than adult-sized. Lenan must have been only the most recent Chosen to meet his end here in Hazror's lair. The Semidragon must have been drawing a skull, a warning from the Codex!

Tal changed the light in his Sunstone from white to red and sent a Red Ray of Destruction blasting out at Hazror's head.

Hazror countered with a Violet Shield of Discontinuity and the Red Ray disappeared into some other, unknown reality. But the Shield only covered his head. Blasting off another ray at his enemy's knees, Tal dived to the ground.

That saved his life. Hazror instantly counter-attacked and a great blast of Indigo light flashed over Tal's head. Tal didn't even know what the spell was, except that it was enormously destructive.

His Red Ray hit Hazror, but several hidden Sunstones flashed round his calves, absorbing the strike. Other stones glittered into life along his arms and thighs.

Tal gasped in shock as an aura of light sprang up all around the creature.

Hazror was literally covered in Sunstones. Hundreds and hundreds of them.

With so many defensive Sunstones, Tal's light attacks were useless.

Hazror was invulnerable.

Tal rolled away as another Indigo blast smoked the ground where he'd been a second ago. He kept on rolling, fear making his mind work faster than it ever had before.

He couldn't run. He'd need time to create walls to hold back the sand.

He couldn't fight Hazror with light.

Hazror laughed. His voice was still Lenan's, though much higher and more shrill.

"Another Chosen come to play, another Chosen come to pay!"

There was only one thing left to do, Tal thought. Something no Chosen would ever think of.

But Tal wasn't only a Chosen now. Whether he wanted to or not, he had learned something of being an Icecarl.

He snapped out of his roll, ducked another blast and threw himself feet-first at Hazror.

The creatures laugh was cut off as Tal's boots crashed into his stomach. He went flying over backwards. A ray of Violet light sprang out of his Sunstone, melting a hole through a wall.

But it missed Tal. He grabbed Hazror's arm and twisted it behind his back. He'd half expected the creature to be enormously strong, but Hazror howled in pain and did not resist.

He did start screaming.

"Arval! Rowthr! Govror!"

At these words, one of the walls of light

suddenly winked out revealing more steps leading down. Bestial roars echoed through the doorway, coming from far below.

Obviously Hazror's servants or guards – or whatever they were – were on their way.

"You will suffer for this!" hissed Hazror as Tal dragged him across to the stairs. "You will suffer!"

Tal didn't answer. He reached around and ripped the chain that held the Sunstones and the whistle from Hazror's neck. The creature screamed and whimpered.

"My neck! You've hurt my neck!"

It was only then that Tal realised that Hazror had no shadow.

He was *not* an Aeniran creature.

He was just a very, very old man. An ancient man. And he must have once been a Chosen. But he had left that behind when he came here. Judging from the bones and the Sunstones, he had lured tens if not hundreds of young Chosen to their deaths.

Tal felt the disgust rise in him. How could anyone do what this man had done? How could he betray his own people?

"You'll suffer," whimpered Hazror. "I'll show you how light can hurt—"

Tal didn't listen to him any more.

He let go.

The old man, poised on the brink of the stairs, suddenly caught his breath and stopped his threats. He teetered there for a moment, arms flailing.

Tal saw glowing red eyes coming up from below. Ferocious eyes, as large as his hands. Vengenarl eyes.

Hazror swung forwards screaming.

Before he could swing back, Tal gave him a push.

17

Milla tried to pass through the door seven times and Odris eighteen. Each and every time they ended up exactly where they'd left.

Milla also tried hacking at the wood, but neither her bone knife nor Merwin-horn sword could even scratch it.

"We'll have to fly off the roof," Milla said finally.

But when they climbed back up they could no more leave the roof than they could the door. Every time Odris launched herself off one side of the tower they found themselves landing on the other side.

They could see out, but they couldn't get there.

"I wonder what happens next," said Milla. She

instinctively knew it was a trap with a purpose. Something would happen soon.

Something lethal, she suspected. Something that had to do with the smell of burning, which was growing stronger as the night wore on.

She paced around the walkway several more times, thinking. Then she said, "Come on," to Odris and went back downstairs.

At the bottom she stood in front of the door and raised her Sunstone. Concentrating on it she called it into full light. Bright white light that filled the bottom level and spilled out into the night.

"I'm here!" yelled Milla to the waiting Nanuch. "Here!"

"What are you doing?" asked Odris anxiously.

"I'm trying to get one to come in," explained Milla. "I might be able to jump out as one jumps in."

"Oh," said Odris. "But what about me?"

"I'll throw one in for you," said Milla.

It was a good plan. But it didn't work because the Nanuch wouldn't come any closer.

Something else did though. A small green lizard

approached the door. It walked upright on its hind legs wearing a harness made from woven grass from which hung a sword no longer than Milla's forefinger. It bore a quiver of tiny arrows on its back, and carried a bow only slightly shorter than it was tall.

"A Kurshken," said Odris. "I wonder what it wants."

The Kurshken came up within a few stretches of the door and bowed. Then it spoke, in a surprisingly deep voice for one so small.

"Greetings, Milla and Odris. I am Quorr Quorr Quorr Ahhtorn Sezicka. You may call me Zicka."

"Greetings," said Milla, bowing in turn. "How do you know our names?"

"The Codex of the Chosen has spoken in my head," said Zicka. "It told me to come here. Soon it will speak through my mouth."

"Do you know how we can get out of here?" asked Milla. "Or does the Codex know?"

Zicka started to speak, then froze. His eyes grew cloudy. Rather like a Crone Mother's, Milla noticed. Then he spoke again and his voice sounded different, the words coming less fluently.

"I am the Codex. I need your help. Tal alone cannot free me. You must meet him. Zicka will show you where."

"What if we don't want to help?" asked Milla. "I see no reason to help any Chosen, least of all Tal. He has betrayed—"

"I have little time to speak thus," interrupted the Codex. "Tal has done what he had to do. If you agree to help, Zicka will free you from the Dawn House. If not, you will die."

"The Dawn House?" asked Milla. "What is—"

Before she could finish the question, Zicka's eyes cleared.

"Well?" he said, his voice normal again. "What is it to be?"

"A Shield Maiden does not barter favours," Milla said angrily. "Free us from this prison. Then I will decide."

"That is not the instruction of the Codex," said Zicka. He looked up at the sky and added, "You had best think quickly. Dawn is not far away."

"What happens at dawn?" asked Odris. "By the way, I'm happy to help anyone who'll help me."

"With the rising of the sun, the Dawn House burns," said Zicka.

"Why?" asked Milla. She shook her head. Nothing in Aenir made sense to her.

"It was not always so," said Zicka. "It is a curse, I suppose. Something left over from the war. Perhaps something hid here, only to be burned out, and the spell continues. The fire only destroys whatever is in the Dawn House. The tower itself is never harmed."

Milla looked at the Sunstone on her finger. She had to get that back to the clan. And there was much information too.

But was it more important than the laws of the Shield Maidens?

A Shield Maiden does not barter favours. But that was only the seventh law. It was not the most important.

Besides, it might be in the interest of all Icecarls for Milla to help Tal return the Codex to the Castle.

Even if he was a traitor to her and had ruined her future, she had to ignore that and think of what was most important to the clans.

The Codex's words also sat in her mind, squatting like unwelcome guests on the deck of an iceship. *Tal has done what he had to do...*

"The first red glow shows on the horizon," said Zicka calmly. "The house will soon begin to burn."

Milla paced across the room, wrestling with the decision. It felt like surrendering and she could never surrender. But was it really?

Tiny tendrils of smoke started to rise up around her feet as she walked. Odris floated closer to the doorway and cleared her throat several times. But she did not speak. The Storm Shepherd could feel the turmoil in Milla, the difficulty of the decision.

Besides, Odris thought, she'd probably survive a fire. It would hurt and she would be spread through every room, but she could probably pull herself back together. Though she would need water immediately afterwards. And that would be difficult if she was still trapped...

"Milla!" Odris said anxiously. "We're on fire!"

Tiny flames were licking up the walls and

the smoke tendrils were winding together into thicker plumes.

Milla ignored smoke, flame and Odris. She went to the door.

"What is it to be?" asked Zicka quickly.

18

Hazror fell down the stairs, screaming all the way. A third of the way down he catapulted straight into the path of his three Vengenarls. All four of them got tangled together and fell another thirty steps.

Tal didn't wait to look. He raced back to where he'd come in. A wall of light blocked the steps to the surface, drowned in sand. Tal had already thought of how to deal with that.

He would make a Hand of Light and use it to carry himself up to the surface.

There was only one slight flaw in this plan. Tal had only ever seen a Hand of Light made once, by three Guards who were all much more experienced light mages than he was. But he had found that making the Stairway of Light in the Pit had opened up his mind to all sorts of Light Magic that he couldn't previously do or hadn't ever known about. Tal was pretty certain he knew how to make a Hand.

Actually there were *two* flaws. The other one was that he had to make the Hand in the few minutes he had before Hazror and the Vengenarls stopped falling down the stairs and came ravening up them instead.

Tal put all those thoughts to the very back of his mind and concentrated on his Sunstone. He had two other stones now, taken from Hazror, but the one in his ring he knew best.

He knew Orange light best too, so it was with that he decided to weave his hand. First of all he sent out a thin beam. He gradually widened that until it was like a band of cloth, which he wove backwards and forwards to build up his Hand.

Because time was short he actually made more of a Mitten than a Hand. It had a thumb, but no fingers. It hovered a stretch away from him, as tall as he was and four times as wide.

Tal concentrated on the Hand. Slowly it drifted towards him. For a moment he thought he'd made it too insubstantial, but when it touched him it felt solid.

The Hand closed with Tal inside it and backed away from the wall of light that covered the exit. Then it rushed forwards, knuckles out, Tal braced inside for the shock.

The Hand hit the wall of light and smashed straight through. Orange light flared and sand started geysering in through the V of the thumb, where there was a slight gap.

Up! thought Tal urgently, his head bent over his Sunstone in intense concentration. *Up!*

The Hand pushed its way through the sand. Tal's Sunstone shone so brightly he had to close his eyes as it pumped power into the Hand.

Behind him sand poured like a tidal wave through the broken wall of light into Hazror's lair. Tal hadn't planned it like that, but the sand was covering his retreat. With his best Sunstones taken, Hazror would be hard put to stem the flow of sand.

He would not be able to pursue immediately.

Tal kept urging the Hand up. Even when it burst out on the surface, flinging sand and slabs of stone in all directions, he kept it going.

He was almost two hundred stretches up in the air when Adras caught up with him and said, "Tal! What are you doing?"

Distracted Tal lost concentration. The Hand rippled from Orange to Yellow and then through the entire spectrum.

"Dark take it!" cursed Tal.

He lost control completely. His Sunstone went dark. The Hand vanished and Tal started to fall.

He didn't start screaming until he was halfway down because he'd thought Adras would catch him.

Unfortunately Adras didn't realise he was needed until it was almost too late. He came diving down and snatched at Tal's hands when the boy was certain he was about to die.

Tal kept screaming after Adras saved him, but this time it was because his arms had been almost pulled out of their sockets.

After a moment he recovered and stopped his

panicked howling. They were still quite high up and there was no sign of movement in the sand below.

"Fly east!" Tal croaked. He could stand the pain in his shoulders a bit longer. "Fly as far as you can."

"Sure," said Adras. He craned his head down to look at his companion. "I guess Hazror wasn"t so bad after all. He gave you one... two... Sunstones. And what's that other thing?"

"I think it's a key," said Tal. He was shivering now, in delayed shock. "And Hazror didn't give it to me, or the Sunstones. That's why we have to fly as far as we can."

"Why?" asked Adras. Then, in a slightly different tone, he added, "Oh. I see. Hazror will want them back."

Then, later still, the Storm Shepherd gingerly asked, "How bad and terrible is he by the way?"

"Very. Both," said Tal. Worse than he'd imagined, because he was not an Aeniran creature.

How could a Chosen become like Hazror? Why did he live like he did, preying on innocent young Chosen?

Then a much nastier thought came to Tal's mind.

How did the young Chosen find Hazror? Why would they go there in the first place? It wasn't as if his lair was easy to locate, or in any well-known place for finding and binding Spiritshadows.

Had they all been sent by the Codex, like he was? Sacrificed to try and get the bone whistle that now hung around his own neck?

Or had someone else sent them to their deaths?

Lenan had been a very smart boy, Tal recalled. He'd graduated first from the Lectorium last year. Maybe he had discovered some of the things that Tal had been finding out.

Tal had a lot of questions. He hoped he'd find the Codex soon and that it could answer some of them.

Even if he was afraid of the answers.

"I will help Tal with the Codex," coughed Milla. The smoke had thickened so fast that she was already choking and she couldn't see Odris at all. Even so, Milla tried to speak slowly and with pride. She was not begging to be saved from the fire.

"Excellent!" said Zicka. "Catch!"

He drew an arrow from his quiver, tied an almost invisible cord of spider silk to it and, with one elegant arch of his arm and back, fired it close to Milla's hand. She caught the arrow easily. Out in the Dark World she had caught bigger arrows that were actually aimed at her. It was a rare skill and another mark of her prowess as a warrior.

"You are connected to the outside now," said Zicka. "Grab hold of Odris and walk slowly outside. Do not break the cord!"

He started stepping backwards, uncoiling more spider silk as he did.

Milla reached behind her and grabbed something soft and squishy that she hoped was Odris. The Storm Shepherd didn't feel like she usually did, but Milla's eyes were streaming so much from the smoke she couldn't see.

Bending down low to find the clearest air she stepped out.

Smoke billowed out with air, but she kept on walking to make sure Odris was completely out as well.

"Good!" cried Zicka. "Now we have to outrun the Nanuch before they wake up."

"Which way?" asked Milla. She could only see out of one tear-swimming eye.

"This way!" shouted Zicka, and he was off. Milla staggered after him, still dragging Odris. The Storm Shepherd was silent.

The amount of smoke that billowed out covered

their escape so that none of the Nanuch noticed they were gone. Even so, Zicka led them at a run through the grey wood for a long time. Milla was gasping from the exertion when the wood suddenly came to an end, the trees stopping all along a perfectly straight line.

Beyond the wood lay an ordered expanse of trimmed hedges and lawns, interspersed with flower beds alive with colour.

Zicka stopped just past the trees.

"We'll rest here," said the Kurshken. "Then we can follow the edge of the forest north. It is best not to go into the Garden."

"Why?" asked Milla. It took an effort to find the breath to speak.

"I don't know," replied Zicka. "Only that anyone who goes past the first row of hedges does not return."

Milla stared out over the perfectly ordered garden. It stretched as far as she could see and looked entirely harmless. There were insects of some kind flying around the flowers and she could see birds in the distance. Small ones that darted in and out of the hedges.

"Are you sure about this?" asked Odris. "I can see a pool not too far in and I do need water."

"I only know that it is not safe. The Codex may know the secret of it," said Zicka. "Or the Hollow Oracle, or the Old Khamsoul. Since we cannot ask any of them, I suggest we simply avoid the place."

"But I really do need a drink," wailed Odris. "Can't I just fly over there a little bit?"

"No!" ordered Milla. Zicka had proved to be truthful about the dangers of the Dawn House. Milla had to presume the Kurshken was also right about the Garden. "I need a drink too, but it isn"t worth risking our lives."

"I bet it's just walking creatures that have to worry," said Odris petulantly. "Look at those birds. They're perfectly all right."

"They are bait," said Zicka, his voice ominous. The lizard started walking along the line of trees, not bothering to check if the others were following.

Milla followed immediately. Odris hesitated, taking one last look at the pool of water just beyond the first hedges. It did look rather too perfect she realised with a shiver, and followed Milla.

They walked north for a long time. The sun was almost directly above them when they came to a broad river – more than two hundred stretches wide – that marked the northern border of the grey forest and the Garden. Beyond the river lay a stony wasteland of sinkholes and terraced hills of stone.

"It is safe to drink here," said Zicka. "I also have food aboard my ship. It is not much for someone your size, Milla—"

"Any food is welcome," interrupted Milla. "But where is your ship?"

Zicka pointed at the river's edge. For a moment Milla couldn't work out what the lizard was pointing at. Then she realised he must mean the partially submerged log that was lying in the shallows.

"That is a ship?" asked Odris. She didn't need to add that it looked like a piece of debris thrown up by the river.

"Come," said Zicka proudly. "I will show you. She is called 'Roquollollollahahinanahbek' in our own tongue, which is to say, 'The Fire of Many Suns on First Blue of Deep Water,' in the shared speech. She is an heirloom of our people, a gift from long ago."

"It's a log," whispered Odris to Milla. "A piece of a tree. The Kurshken's mad."

"Quiet!" ordered Milla.

The lizard jumped down to the log and ran along its length. Milla stopped at the shore. One end of the log was buried under mud and earth. There was no chance that this log could be pushed out into the river to make even a raft.

Then Zicka bent down and put his head underwater. Bubbles came up and Milla heard a burbling noise.

The Kurshken was talking underwater.

For a moment Milla was in agreement with Odris. The lizard was mad.

The moment passed quickly. For as Zicka pulled his head out of the water, there was a disturbance in the middle of the river. Ripples suddenly spread where the water had been calm.

A mast shot up out of the water, a slender pole that was quickly followed by a carved bow and stern and then an entire ship. Water gushed off and out of it as it rose and the bow turned to the shore where Zicka was waiting.

Milla stared. The ship, apart from its lack of runners, was an exact replica of a small Icecarl iceship of the kind called an Orskir. It was a three- or four-person vessel that a Sword-Thane might have, or a Shield Maiden messenger. It even had similar carvings on its bow and stern, whorls and curves that mimicked cloud and wind.

Its hull was not bone, or even wood, as might be expected on this world. It was metal, the same deep golden metal that the Ruin Ship was made from. But it was also set with many Sunstones, hundreds and hundreds of them that glittered in the sunlight.

Milla found herself kneeling on the log. She knew this ship from the tales told by the Crones when the whole clan was huddled in the hold, while the worst of the winter storms howled about the many-times-anchored vessel.

This was Asteyr's ship. Asteyr, the mother of Danir and Susir and Grettir, who in turn were the foremothers of all the clans. But in the stories the Orskir of Asteyr travelled on ice. What was it doing here in Aenir, on a river, in the possession of a lizard?

"Asteyr's ship," croaked Milla. "How... how did your people come by this?"

"Yes, yes," replied Zicka, his purple tongue flickering. "It was Asteyr's ship, in the faraway times. We did her a service, but the ship was given to us later from the hands of her daughter Danir. That is why we agreed to the Codex's request – to help a daughter of Danir."

"What service?" asked Milla, still staring in awe at the ship. "What did you do?"

"I cannot say, even to a daughter of Danir," said Zicka. "It is a secret of our folk. I cannot speak of it without the permission of the Kurshken Allthing."

The fabled ship had drifted up to the log. Zicka leaped up and gripped the gunwale, then vaulted over. Milla climbed up reverently and stood upon the deck.

The ship was completely dry and there were no pools of water, nothing to show that it had been submerged. Milla stood near the bow, strangely afraid to go further, to walk where Asteyr and Danir had once walked. She felt like she should clean her boots, or change her clothes, or something.

Odris drifted across above her and settled around the mast, rather like a sail. There was no sail, nor boom, nor any of the rigging that Milla would have expected of an iceship. There was also no wheel or steering oar. Nevertheless, the ship swung out into the river and began to move.

"Where do we go?" asked Milla. But Zicka had moved to the stern and didn't hear her. Reluctantly, Milla tiptoed towards him, keeping close to the rail.

"Where do we go?" she repeated.

"Four Rivers Meet," said Zicka. "Close by Cold Stone Mountain. The Chosen Tal should be there too, all being well."

20

Tal's shoulder sockets hurt so much he wanted to land long before Adras got tired of carrying him. By then they were already well beyond the sand dunes of Hazror's realm. The country below them was now a jungle, a canopy of green, broken here and there by taller trees thrusting out.

Under the starlight the canopy looked black rather than green. It reminded Tal of the Veil and the Seven Towers, which was comforting. But it made it difficult to land. Tal kept thinking he could see a clearing, but it was always a trick of the light, just a dip in the canopy.

Tal thought his arms were actually going to fall

off when he finally saw a large expanse that had to be a clearing.

Adras landed him gently, but Tal still fell over. All his muscles hurt, not just his shoulders. Even so, he forced himself up out of the wet leaf-litter. There was no time to rest. Now that he had the whistle he felt closer to the Codex somehow. But that only increased his anxiety. What if he found the Codex and found out who was keeping Gref captive, but it was too late?

Tal got up and looked around, raising light from his Sunstone.

He was in a clearing, but the leaf-litter was still knee-deep. There were shrubs and ferns almost as tall as he was, but none of the enormous, vine-circled trees that filled the jungle proper.

"I like it here," boomed Adras suddenly, making Tal jump. "Lots of moisture in the air. Ahhh!"

Tal didn't like it so much. There were lots of things moving in the darkness. He could hear squelching and crackling and slithering, though whenever he shined the beam of light from his Sunstone there was nothing to be seen.

Even worse than that he'd suddenly remembered the last game of Beastmaker he'd played, and one of the cards. The Jarghoul, the giant strangling snake of the Aeniran jungle.

This was the Aeniran jungle. This was exactly where you could expect to find a thirty-stretch-long Jarghoul that would be thicker than he was tall.

It could be a Jarghoul making those slithering noises over there!

Tal spun around, intensifying the light from his Sunstone.

Light reflected back from two enormous, pale yellow eyes. Eyes that bulged on stalks above slimy blue flesh that continued to glow even when Tal's shaking hand moved the light away.

"Jarghoul!" Tal screamed, and he turned to run.

He'd gone several steps when his panicked brain properly processed what he'd seen.

It wasn't a Jarghoul. They weren't blue and they didn't glow in the dark.

It was a Gorblag, a sort of slithering toad. Or at the worst, its close cousin, a Klorbag, which spat disgusting but harmless slimeballs.

"A what?" asked Adras. "Do you want me to smack it?"

"Ah, no," said Tal, after he took a deep breath. "It's... it's only a Gorblag. They're harmless."

The glowing blue toad hadn't moved. It just sat there, its long-finned tail slithering from side to side. Then it slowly inflated the fleshy bags under its stomach and became twice as large.

Tal got out of the direct line of fire in case it was a Klorbag preparing to spit.

It didn't. Its eyes clouded and its mouth pursed in a way that no Gorblag's mouth had ever pursed before. Then its airbags started to deflate and a whistle came out of its mouth.

Tal had already realised it had been taken over by the Codex. Even so he was surprised that the whistle was actually a reedy, high-pitched voice.

"What is it?" he asked. "What do you want me to do?"

"Tal. Aim one hand left of the blue star and fly. Milla at Four Rivers Meet by dawn. Follow Zicka to Cold Stone Mountain. Have a Storm Shepherd blow the Pipe. You and Milla fetch me from under the Mountain. No Aeniran can touch me. Go now!"

"What?" asked Tal. "But Milla will kill me!"

"No!" the Gorblag whistled. "Go! Four Rivers Meet. Zicka. Cold Stone Mountain. Blow Pipe. Fetch Codex from under Mountain."

"Milla *will* kill me," protested Tal. "And how am I going to get under the mountain?"

It was too late. The Codex had lost contact. The Gorblag's eyes cleared. It stopped pursing its lips and opened its mouth wide. An instant later a huge gob of sticky, foul-smelling slime whizzed past Tal's face.

The Klorbag dived down into the leaf-litter and squirmed away before Tal or Adras could retaliate. Tal watched its dorsal fin snaking through the rotting vegetation to make sure it wasn't going to turn for a parting shot.

Then he held up his hands.

"We've got to get going again," he said to Adras. "The Codex wants us to go to somewhere called Four Rivers Meet. And it has somehow got Milla to help."

"Milla?" asked Adras eagerly. "The other one? With Odris?"

"Yes," said Tal. "We have to aim a hand's width left of the blue star, so once we're up out of this jungle I guess I'll have to hang by one arm and try—"

He stopped talking as it was obvious Adras wasn't listening. He had reared up and had his head cocked to one side, as if he were listening to something that Tal couldn't hear.

"Find Odris, find Milla," the Storm Shepherd announced. "That's right?"

"Yes." Tal sighed. "If you know where Odris is."

"I know." Adras bent down and gripped Tal's forearms, not noticing the boy wince with pain. "The wind tells me."

"Good," said Tal faintly. His shoulder sockets felt like they'd had molten metal poured inside them and the pain was spreading through to his neck and head. But the Codex had said to go on and so he must.

As Adras rose up out of the jungle, Tal's thoughts turned to Milla. He hoped the Codex had told her she wasn't going to kill him.

He also felt the slight twinge of guilt he'd had previously grow stronger inside him.

Tal still thought he'd done the right thing. The only thing. But now he was wondering if Milla could ever see it his way. Maybe making her swap her shadow for a Spiritshadow was like a Chosen not having a Spiritshadow.

Maybe... maybe he'd turned her into a sort of Icecarl Underfolk.

He'd really destroyed her future he realised, when all *he'd* given up was his *choice* of Spiritshadow.

She would want to kill him, Tal decided. But he couldn't let her, because right now saving Gref and his family was more important than anything else.

No matter what it cost.

21

It took Tal and Adras all night to fly to Four Rivers Meet. They had to make frequent stops for Tal to massage his arms and rotate his shoulders. Eventually Adras had to actually carry Tal, the Storm Shepherd's arms wrapped completely round the Chosen boy. It was somewhat humiliating, but Tal had long since given up caring about that. He was merely glad that it didn't hurt.

They sighted Four Rivers Meet shortly after dawn. At least Tal presumed that's what it was. Certainly he could see four rivers flowing in from north, south, east and west, to meet in a crazy four-way delta of black mud and thousands of channels that made no sense to Tal.

How could four rivers all flow *into* the same patchwork of channels? The four deltas should end in a lake, but they didn't. At least one of the rivers should be flowing the other way. But none did.

The rivers just kept on spreading and dividing, their many fingers stretching across a wide plain. A completely flat plain, Tal thought at first. But then as the sun rose higher he saw that there was something in the very middle of the delta.

A mountain, surrounded on all sides by narrow streams and reedy islets.

None of it made sense. The water from the four rivers had to go somewhere. But the mountain was sitting where a lake should be.

Tal looked away and blinked and then looked back. But everything was still there. A huge mass of grey stone in the middle of a vast channel system that couldn't possibly work.

That's Aenir, Tal told himself. *Aeniran Magic.*

"Odris!" Adras exclaimed. He started to point, but remembered that he was cradling Tal and stopped.

Tal looked down. There was a ship below them moving quite quickly along one of the larger channels. It sparkled in the morning sun and Tal's trained eye picked up the glint of Sunstones. Many Sunstones.

He could see a dot on the deck that he presumed was Milla and Odris was quite clearly the cloud that was twined about the mast. There was something else moving on deck too, something small. Tal couldn't see what it was at that distance.

Adras started to descend. Tal closed his eyes and tried to think of what he was going to say to Milla. Would it help if he apologised? Did Icecarls apologise? Or would she just think less of him?

Should he try and stun her with a Blue Slap before she could do anything to him?

He wasn't afraid exactly. He just felt terrible. No matter how he tried, he simply couldn't think of Milla as someone whose life didn't matter.

Then he felt a bump as if they'd hit something solid and he opened his eyes. They hadn't hit anything, but Adras was suddenly climbing very quickly.

"Adras!" Tal shouted in sudden panic. "What are

you doing? We're supposed to be going down!"

"Updraft!" Adras boomed. "A hot air current too strong for me to fly against. I am only a cloud."

"What!" Tal screamed. Desperately he tried to think of something he could do. They were rising so rapidly that he was beginning to feel faint. They must already be thousands of stretches up, as high as the Seven Towers back on the Dark World. Far too high to build a Stairway of Light.

"How do we get down?" he shouted.

"When the air cools, we will fall," Adras roared. "Have patience!"

"But I can't breathe!" gasped Tal.

Adras was silent. Tal had already noticed that his Storm Shepherd companion had trouble when he had to think new thoughts or consider how other beings lived.

Cool air, he thought. Somehow he had to make the air cooler. But how? He could make it hotter with his Sunstone, but not cooler.

Then it came to him.

"Adras!" he shouted. The shout took most of his breath and the next words came out as little more than a whisper. "Rain! Rain will make it cooler!"

"What?"

"Rain!"

"Ah! Rain!" bellowed Adras. He swung his arms forwards so quickly that Tal thought he was about to be thrown off into space. But he was only shifting him out of the way. The rest of his cloud-body roiled and rippled, spreading out into a broad circular shape and becoming even puffier.

The cloud grew blacker. Tal rolled on to his side so he could see. He could already smell the fresh scent of rain and the temperature dropped several degrees.

It got colder still and there was a hideous grinding noise inside the Storm Shepherd. Tal saw flecks of white appearing in the darkness of the cloud. Then large chunks of ice started to fall.

Very large chunks of ice. In fact, gigantic hailstones the size of Tal's head. Some were thrown out at a sharp angle, narrowly missing the boy as he twisted and turned in the Storm Shepherd's arms.

With the hailstones, the temperature dropped to freezing. Slowly at first, the Storm Shepherd began to fall.

"I said rain!" shouted Tal as they fell faster and faster. "Milla's down there somewhere, you idiot! She could get killed by a hailstone!"

Then the cold really took effect and cloud and boy dropped as fast as the hailstones.

"Soooooooooorrrrrrrrrryyyyyyy!" boomed Adras.

"Slow down!" shrieked Tal. But his voice was lost in the rush of their descent. He was shivering uncontrollably now, the chill of the wind making the icy temperature even lower. He felt as cold as he ever had out on the Ice.

But now he had a Sunstone, Tal thought. Several in fact. He hadn't really had time to examine the ones he'd taken from Hazror and he wasn't going to start while he was dropping like a stone from the sky.

Tal held out his hand. His fingers were already blue and he could hardly feel them. But the Sunstone glinted there. He focused on it, willing it to warm the air around his body.

At first he thought he'd failed. It was one of the simplest spells that almost any Chosen child could perform with a Sunstone. But he was still freezing.

Then he realised that he just couldn't feel the

heat because the cold was so intense. He'd have to increase the amount of heat the Sunstone put out.

He concentrated again and felt a wave of heat come off the top of the Sunstone and blow back around him. Some went into Adras as well.

They were still falling almost straight down. Tal risked a look, but his eyes instantly filled with tears from the rushing wind. Even through teary eyes he could see that the river was very close.

Tal told the Sunstone to put out even more heat, but there was a limit to the amount it could radiate outwards without heating up the ring and burning his finger. Waves of hot air billowed off it, but it was not enough to counteract the cold.

"Haaaaannnngggg oooonnnnnn!" yelled Adras, and the Storm Shepherd reared back. Their vertical descent turned into a long glide. They were still dropping, but it now looked like there was a slight chance they would pull up before smacking into a channel or one of the muddy islands.

But they didn't.

Adras roared and Tal shouted as the water loomed closer and closer. Tal just had time to take a deep breath, a breath that was knocked out of him a second later as they hit the water.

Storm Shepherd and Chosen boy went under, a long way underwater and actually into the mud of the river floor.

Tal found himself trapped not only by Adras's arms, but also by sticky mud that refused to let go. He couldn't breathe and he couldn't see. He flailed his arms and his legs as he tried to break free.

His whole mind was filled with panic. He just wanted to take a breath. He had to breathe. He had to suck something into his lungs.

Even if it was water.

22

Milla and Odris saw Adras and Tal hit the water about two hundred stretches in front of them, sending up a plume of spray higher than the ship's mast.

Milla rushed to the bow and climbed up to look out. As the spray subsided she expected to see Tal's head bob up and a cloud emerge. But there were only the ripples of the impact.

Milla hesitated. She felt that she should dive in, but she was not a strong swimmer. Icecarls did not swim unless the Ice broke, in which case they had less than two minutes to get out of the water anyway.

"Odris!" she called. "Help them!"

"What for?" asked Odris. "Adras will work out what to do before too long. What an idiot! I couldn't believe it when I saw the hail. You'd never know he was the older of the pair of us and that by two hundred years."

"Tal will drown!" shouted Milla. "Go and help!"

"He can't live underwater?" asked Odris, shocked. She suddenly launched off the mast and shot over Milla's head. A moment later there was another, smaller plume of spray as the second Storm Shepherd plunged into the water.

Milla watched anxiously. For all his faults, Tal didn't deserve to drown.

A few air bubbles burst on the surface of the river, then one very heavy-looking Storm Shepherd emerged, lurching up to hang only a few stretches above the water. Milla couldn't tell which one it was, till it reached down and dragged another one up, who held Tal in its dripping arms.

The Chosen boy was covered in mud, but he was alive, judging by the coughing and spluttering Milla could hear.

Asteyr's boat moved up close to the bedraggled Storm Shepherds and their human cargo. Adras was about to put Tal on board when Milla cried out.

"Wait! He's too muddy! Rinse him off first!"

Adras immediately complied, dunking Tal back into the river. The Chosen boy only just had time to shout, "No!" before he was completely submerged yet again.

Tal was lifted out spitting, coughing and furious. Dropped on to the deck, he tried to get up to shout at Milla, but he was taken by a fit of coughing. Too weak to rise, he tried to crawl away from Milla. But he had only gone half a stretch when she grabbed him.

For a second he thought she was going to throw him over the side. Then he realised she was helping him up so he could vomit up water over the gunwale.

And she wasn't screaming death threats at him. She was just telling him to be careful he wasn't sick on the boat.

Even when no more water seemed likely to come up, Tal kept hanging over the side. He felt as limp and washed out as an old Underfolk mop.

But at least he was alive. And Milla hadn't tried to kill him. Even if she was being extremely weird about messing up this riverboat.

"So," croaked Tal. "We meet again."

"Yes," said Milla coldly. "Traitor. I have not forgotten. However, I have agreed to help find your Codex and return it to the Dark World. I will return to my people too, to tell them what I have learned of Aenir and the Chosen's folly. After that, I will give myself to the Ice."

"What?" asked Tal. "What's the Chosen's folly?"

"Do not pretend you do not know," said Milla scornfully. "I have learned that the Veil was made to keep Aenirans out of our world. It is you Chosen who have broken faith with our ancestors, bringing Spiritshadows back to the Castle. You have let the Aenirans establish a foothold on our world once more."

"What are you talking about?" asked Tal. He felt dizzy and his head was clogged with water. "We have always had Spiritshadows; we have always come to Aenir for them. The Veil has nothing to do with it."

"That is not correct," said a voice Tal hadn't heard before. He lifted himself off the gunwale with effort and turned to see who it was. He hadn't expected it to be a Kurshken. He knew from the Beastmaker game that the lizards were very smart, but he didn't know they could talk.

"I am Quorr Quorr Quorr Ahhtorn Sezicka. You may call me Zicka. As with so many of my kind, I am a historian. As such I can inform you that you are quite incorrect. The Chosen first started coming to Aenir for the purposes of taking slaves – whom you term Spiritshadows – less than nine hundred years ago. Prior to that there was a period of more than a thousand years when there was no communication between the Dark World and Aenir. This was due to the ban on travelling between the two worlds that was established by Asteyr and Ramellan after the creation of the Veil on your world and the execution of the Forgetting in ours."

"What?" Tal asked again. He felt like this was the only word he knew how to say. Then he got angry. What was he doing listening to a lizard and a savage? They knew nothing of the Chosen and the Castle and its history.

"I don't know where you heard these stories," Tal said. "But I know that we have always had Spiritshadows. We have always come to Aenir for them. That is what Aenirans are for!"

"Always?" questioned Zicka. "That is not a specific measurement of time. And you think this whole world exists purely for the purpose of providing Chosen with Spiritshadows?"

Tal was silent. He didn't know how to answer that question. He didn't feel strong enough to debate it. While he would never admit it to Milla or this Zicka lizard, he knew that his knowledge of Chosen, Castle, Dark World and Aenir was severely limited.

"The Codex knows the true history," Tal said finally. "You'll see when we get the Codex."

Zicka smiled. At least Tal thought that was what it was doing with its mouth. Milla frowned. Before she could say anything Tal spoke again.

"Zicka. The Codex mentioned you. You are to take us to Cold Stone Mountain. Then I have to get one of the Storm Shepherds to blow this whistle—"

Tal's hand went to his pocket to pull out the chain with the two Sunstones and the bone whistle he'd taken from Hazror. But when the chain came out, there was nothing on it.

"No!" exclaimed Tal. He dropped the chain and started frantically turning out his pockets. "I had the whistle... and two Sunstones... Gref..."

23

Tal's hand closed on something wedged across the bottom of his pocket. He brought it out with a huge sigh of relief. It was the bone whistle. But there was no sign of the two Sunstones. They had been washed out and were now somewhere on the bottom of the river. Fortunately his own Sunstone ring was secure on his finger.

"I've lost two Sunstones," Tal said mournfully.

But at least he had the whistle. That was the key to gaining the Codex and saving Gref. That was all he could think about now. The rest about the Veil and Aenir was too much.

Use the whistle. Get the Codex. Return to the

Dark World. Find and save Gref.

It was like a light chant that Tal said over and over in his mind.

"The whistle is essential," said Zicka, indicating the bone instrument. "It is the device that will make the mountain move. As long as it continues to sound the mountain will arch its back. While it does, Tal, you and Milla must rush under its belly and bring the Codex out."

"A Storm Shepherd would be faster," said Milla. She was thinking as she would for a hunt or a battle. "And stronger. How heavy is the Codex?"

Zicka's tongue flicked out in a Kurshken negative. Realising that this meant nothing to the others, he quickly said, "No. The Codex cannot be touched by any creature of Aenir. That is part of its protection. As to its size, I believe that it can shrink and grow at will, within certain limits. But its weight remains the same."

"Which is?" asked Milla.

"Fairly heavy," said the Kurshken. "I do not know your measurements of weight. But perhaps the same as Tal."

Tal shook his head. He didn't feel up to walking fifty stretches, let alone running under a lifting mountain to bring out something that weighed as much as he did.

"How far will we have to go?" asked Milla. "And how long can Odris… or Adras… blow the whistle?"

"I believe about five ship lengths," said Zicka, indicating the distance from stern to bow with his arms. "And I do not know how long the whistle can be sounded."

Odris peered down at the bone whistle.

"Days I should think," she said. "Unless it's magical."

"It *is* magical," Tal said wearily. "Otherwise it wouldn't move a mountain."

"Let me try it now," said Odris.

She took the whistle and raised it to her mouth. But no sound came out when she blew. Her cheeks bulged out further and further until she looked rather like a Gorblag. But still no sound came from the whistle.

"It has been made for a single purpose and can only be used near the mountain," said Tal with confidence. Aenir was full of magical items that only worked in certain circumstances or particular places. "Though I hope you can blow it there. Maybe Adras should do it. He can probably hold his breath longer."

"No he can't!" said Odris.

"Yes I can!" growled Adras. "Let's have a competition."

Both started to suck in air, requiring Tal, Milla and Zicka to move sternwards to avoid being pulled over.

Tal started to sit down with his back to the mast, but Milla jerked him back up.

"Don't! You'll get the deck wet!"

Tal angrily shrugged her hand off. Milla stepped back and Tal saw the familiar spread of her fingers that meant she was about to reach for her sword.

"I'm tired!" he yelled. "I've just been almost drowned! All I want to do is sit down. Cut my throat if you like, but that'll make even more of a mess of your precious boat!"

He sat down. Milla clenched her teeth and drew her fist back as if she had taken Tal seriously and was going to hit him with that instead of a weapon, so as not to make him bleed. But Zicka plucked at her wrist.

"Do not fight!" the Kurshken said. "Roquollollolla-hahinanahbek has had wet and muddy decks, even bloody ones, before – and will again. She is a working ship, not a relic of the past."

Milla scowled and turned away.

"Thanks," said Tal. "But if this is your boat, why is Milla so upset?"

"This ship," Zicka corrected, "once belonged to the most famous ancestress of Milla – Asteyr, who with Ramellan ended the war between the worlds."

"Who?" asked Tal. "What war?"

"Ask your Codex," replied Zicka. "Since you will doubt whatever I tell you."

"I will." Tal hesitated and then added, "Whose boat did you say this was?"

"Asteyr's," said Zicka.

"And what was the other name you mentioned? You said Asteyr and someone else ended some war?"

"Ramellan. Do you recognise the name?"

Once again, Tal didn't answer. He did recognise the

name now. Ramellan was some sort of important Chosen from the dim past. He couldn't remember exactly why he was important. He was some sort of Emperor before the Chosen had Emperors, Tal thought. A name mentioned in passing in a history lesson and nothing more.

Zicka stood by as if expecting Tal to ask more questions, but the Chosen boy was saved by a sudden shout from Milla.

"The Mountain! Dead ahead!"

Tal wearily stood up and looked ahead. Sure enough there was a grey mountain rising out of the many channels and islands ahead of them. It was still some distance away, a few hours sailing at least.

"So there it is," said Tal. "Do you know if the mountain is guarded?"

"No," replied Zicka. "I know only what the Codex has chosen to share with my forebrain."

"Your what?"

"Forebrain," said Zicka, tapping the lump between his rather poppy eyes. "We Kurshken have two brains. The forebrain is the animal mind, but we also have the 'ërorquialosschurr' or afterbrain.

The Codex can project its thought into my forebrain and I can communicate with it from my afterbrain, or let the Codex use my forebrain to control my voice."

Tal tried to suppress a shudder. He didn't like the idea of having two brains. What if one of them didn't agree with the other one?

"So there could be guards," Tal said. "Though I suppose whoever put the Codex there wouldn't expect anyone to get the whistle from Hazror."

"Whether there are guards there now or not, all of Aenir will soon know if Cold Stone Mountain moves," said Zicka. "You must be prepared to flee as soon as you have the Codex."

"We'll take it back to the Castle," agreed Tal. "But I'll have to find somewhere I know to make the crossing safe. Where is the Chosen Enclave from here?"

"South," said Zicka. "A few days travel, walking. Do you have to go there?"

Tal shook his head.

"No. But I have to be somewhere I know. If the Enclave is a few days south, does that mean the

Sunken Stone Circle is somewhere near here?"

"Yes. Southeast. You could probably reach there by sundown, at a brisk pace. But that ring of stones is no place to be after dark."

"Yes," Tal agreed. "But I have been to the Sunken Stone Circle several times before so I know it well enough to use it as a crossing point."

He looked up at the bow to where Milla was standing, shading her eyes to watch the river and the mountain ahead. Despite the sun, she cast no shadow.

"I'd better... I'd better make my peace with Milla," Tal said, as he stared at the sunshine on the deck. He felt sick at what he'd done to her now, but he would never admit that.

He approached her slowly, all too aware of the Merwin-horn sword at her side and her acute reflexes. When he was four or five stretches away and possibly out of reach of a sudden lunge, he stopped.

After a moment Milla turned to face him. He saw hatred in her eyes, and flinched.

"Milla," he said, unconscious that he was holding his hands out to the Icecarl, as if he begged something from her. "I... wanted to say..."

"Your words are nothing," said Milla. "They are the mist that is parted by the ship, the ice chips under my skates, the blood that drips from day-old Selski meat."

Tal gulped. This was even harder than he thought. He couldn't believe he was trying to apologise to someone who was so alien to him. He felt strangely inferior standing here before her. She seemed taller somehow, the Sunstone ring on her finger flaming in the sunlight, the Merwin-horn sword bright too. More like a Chosen of legend than anything else.

"I'm... I'm sorry," Tal said. He was shaking as he spoke and there were tears glistening in his eyes, tears that were made as much of anger and guilt as they were of sorrow. "I didn't know... I just had to do it... My father told me I had to look after the family, that I had to do *whatever* it took to keep them safe. Whatever it took, and what it was was my shadow and your shadow too, and I didn't even think what it would mean to you. And it was my fault that Gref climbed after me and got taken and I *have* to find him and get him back. He's only nine and there's Kusi as well, and Mother... That's why I did it, that's why... Can you understand... can you..."

His voice trailed off.

Milla did not answer, but her eyes were no longer full of hate. Then she looked away out over the water and said, "Some of my people believe there is a great Reckoner of all Icecarl lives, a place where every hunt and battle is played out upon a vast board, where every birth and death, victory and defeat can be seen. There must have been a small carving there once, one of the smallest, of Selski bone or Merwin rib, that was Milla of the Far Raiders. But that piece has left the board now and plays a different game of life. I do not know the hands that move me now. All I know is that I am not what I was."

There was another, longer silence, then Tal said, "Nor am I."

"Who knows what either of us will become," said Milla. She hesitated. "I understand why you sold my shadow, Tal of the Chosen. But I do not forget.

And it is not the nature of an Icecarl to forgive."

Tal nodded slowly, though he wasn't sure what she meant.

"I cannot kill you," said Milla. "We have shared too much blood and I understand too well why you have done what you did. One day you too may lose your future at the hands of someone you thought a friend."

24

They beached Asteyr's ship on a strip of black mud in the shadow of the mountain and walked up to the very edge of the stony monolith.

It wasn't a particularly big mountain, but it seemed larger than it really was to Tal when he considered that he was going to have to run underneath it. There was an awful lot of rock that would come crushing down if Adras couldn't keep blowing the whistle.

Adras had won the breath-blowing competition, though both Storm Shepherds had managed to blow their breath for hours. This was very encouraging to Tal. He'd thought they might only have minutes to get the Codex out.

"This is the place," announced Zicka, pointing up to where a thick vein of black stone ran through the grey rock, rather like a dark lightning bolt. "The Codex is straight ahead, about five ship lengths in."

"A hundred and thirty stretches," said Milla. She took off her sword and laid it down, then shrugged off her Selski-hide breastplate and threw it down too.

Tal looked up the mountain and then back towards the river and the ship. He felt certain that whoever had put the Codex here would have also left guards or wards, or some protective magic. But he could see nothing. There was no movement on the mountain, in the sky or on the river.

That just made him more suspicious. There should have been birds or insects or something. But there was just a light breeze, whispering through the reeds behind them.

"I am ready," announced Milla. She stretched her arms above her head and lifted her legs and shook them. Tal saw that they were marked with mottled bruises, but he knew enough about Milla now not to ask.

"There is only one thing I want to know before we run," said Milla.

"What?" asked Tal.

"Why is your hair green?"

"A creature vomited on it," said Tal wearily.

Milla smiled, but she did not laugh. Tal thought she would have laughed before he'd given away her shadow.

In addition to the green hair, Tal's shoulders still hurt and he was damp. Fortunately his legs were in fine shape, apart from slightly burned feet.

There was no reason to delay. But he still hesitated, until Milla stopped her stretching and looked at him.

Tal knew that look. She was thinking he wasn't brave enough to go ahead.

"I'm ready too," he said. "Adras? You know what to do?"

"Sure!" boomed the Storm Shepherd. "I just blow in the whistle. Like this."

He raised the whistle and started to blow before anyone could stop him.

A single pure note, almost too high to hear, came

out of the whistle. It seemed to come from all directions, not just from the actual whistle. Echoes came back, multiplying the sound.

It grew louder and louder and as the sound increased the mountain moved.

It started with a rumbling deep in the earth and a vibration that rattled every bone in Tal's legs before travelling up into his teeth. Pebbles and clumps of dirt fell from the mountain's sides, followed by shrubs and trees whose roots were shivered loose as the pockets of dirt they grew in were shrugged off the mountain's back.

Tal saw Adras look surprised. The Storm Shepherd hesitated a little and the note faltered.

"Keep blowing!" screamed Tal.

The Storm Shepherd nodded and kept blowing. The note steadied and grew even stronger.

There was a mighty crack and a curtain of dust and earth exploded everywhere along the mountain's length. Tal and Milla shielded their eyes with their forearms and gingerly edged forwards.

As the cloud of dust cleared they saw that the mountain was rising out of the earth. They could see daylight on the other, distant side, a gap only a stretch high. But the mountain continued to arch back and the gap increased.

"Go!" shouted Zicka. "Go!"

Tal and Milla rushed forwards, hunched over, running as fast as they could through the falling dust and over broken ground.

Milla counted steps as she ran, calling out every ten. One of her paces was close enough to a stretch. At 120 or so they should be able to see the Codex.

They ran on, into the deeper shadow directly under the mountain's belly. It was so close that Tal could have jumped up and touched rock. But he didn't care about that. All his attention was on finding the Codex.

"One hundred!" shouted Milla.

"There it is!" Relief filled Tal's voice.

He pointed up at a hole just ahead. There was a rectangle of silver light up there, bright here in the darkness.

They ran to it. Tal jumped up, but could not get a grip. He fell back. Before he could jump again, Milla used his back and shoulders as a vaulting board. She got up easily and reached an arm back down to pull Tal up.

"Is that the Codex?" gasped Milla, pointing at the luminous slab.

The silver rectangle flashed and letters appeared on it. Tal read the words without realising it.

Yes, I am the Codex. Take me and run! Run! Run! Run!

Tal gripped one side of the Codex as Milla grabbed the other. Both of them looked down and realised that the mountain was still rising. They would have to jump down at least six stretches now, or wait till the mountain started to lower itself again. But that would invite being crushed on the way back!

They lifted the Codex and jumped.

At that exact moment the mountain lurched itself up even higher.

Tal and Milla landed hard on their hands and knees and dropped the Codex.

Pain blossomed in Tal's left shoulder and he cried out.

"Ahhh! My shoulder!"

"Swap sides!" Milla yelled, running around to get her hands under the Codex. "Use your right hand. It's not that heavy." She looked across and saw that Tal's left arm was hanging down much lower than it should. It was obviously dislocated, but she did not have time to push it back in place.

Tal bit back a sob and staggered around. He couldn't move his left arm at all and he presumed it was broken in several places or something equally terrible. But it took only one glance at the vast expanse of rock above to make him get his right hand under the Codex and lift.

"Go! Go!" shouted Milla. They started running again, a clumsy run with the door-sized Codex between them.

They were halfway back to sunshine and safety when the whistle stopped. At exactly the same time the mountain stopped rising.

"Faster!" Milla shouted.

Tal screamed something too, though he didn't know what it was. Every step was agony in his shoulder and he could barely keep a grip on the Codex with his good hand.

With a rumble that deafened them the mountain started to settle back down. It lowered itself in sudden lurches and with frightening quickness. This was no slow and steady relaxation back into its own bed.

Tal saw Zicka in the narrowing band of sunlight ahead of them. The lizard was jumping up and down, screaming something too. Adras and Odris were shouting. Milla was shouting. Everyone was shouting.

Then they heard the top of the Codex scrape on stone. A horrifying sound, even though it only lasted the second it took them to crouch even lower as they ran.

Thirty stretches... twenty stretches... the top of the Codex scraped again and they were carrying it almost horizontally and neither could stand upright without hitting their heads... ten stretches and they were crawling and screaming with the stone pressing on their backs... five stretches... four stretches... their clothes were rubbing on stone... two stretches and then...

25

Their heads were suddenly in sunshine and the Storm Shepherds were dragging them out with the Codex between them. For a terrible second it seemed that the mountain had closed on their feet. And then they were free.

"My shoulder, my shoulder!" Tal cried, half laughing with relief at having got out and half crying with pain from his arm.

Milla stepped up to him, placed one hand on his shoulder and gripped his arm with her other hand.

"Ow! No!" shrieked Tal. "I said I was sorry! Don't torture—"

Milla did something with both hands and there

was a loud click as Tal's arm went back in his shoulder socket. Almost instantly the pain lessened to a dull ache.

"Oh!" said Tal, moving it experimentally. "Thanks."

"Dislocated," said Milla. She turned to Adras and grabbed a chunk of cloud roughly where his chest would be.

"What happened to you?" she asked fiercely, twisting the cloud-flesh. "Why did you stop blowing?"

"I didn't!" protested Adras. "I kept blowing, but no sound came out. It just stopped!"

"That's true," said Zicka.

Milla let go of the Storm Shepherd and quickly shrugged her armour back on. She didn't even seem to be out of breath, Tal noticed. But he felt a strange gladness in his heart. It was good to be back with Milla again when it came to things like escaping from under a settling mountain.

"We have to get away from here," he said urgently as he bent down to pick up the Codex. Milla finished tying her sword scabbard back on her belt and bent to help him.

"I wonder how long it was under there," Milla

said as she picked up her side of the Codex. It seemed a bit larger than it had been under the mountain. She was sure that it had been both thinner and less tall, though it was still about as wide as a door in the Castle.

As Milla spoke, letters formed on the surface of the Codex, black against the silver luminosity.

22 years, 23 days, 14 hours, 3 minutes and 42 seconds.

"What does it say?" asked Milla. The letters were from the Chosen alphabet.

Even as Tal repeated the answer, the letters changed to Icecarl runes. Milla peered at them. She was not a great reader, but she had no trouble with numbers.

"Who put you there?" asked Tal.

Two Chosen carried me in. They were Julper Yen-Baren of the Fifth Indigo and Crislo Hane-Arrit of the Second Violet.

Tal was about to describe the Spiritshadow that took his brother Gref away and ask which Chosen commanded it, but Zicka got in before him.

"I greet you, Mighty Codex," he said. "If you were

to give advice to us now, what would it be?"

Flee. Those who put me here watch carefully. We must return to the Castle. I must not be recaptured by the minions of Skerrako.

"Skerrako?" asked Tal. But he didn't get an answer. Milla was already lifting up her side, so he had to follow suit. Whatever words appeared on the surface of the Codex were seen only by the Storm Shepherds and neither of them could read Chosen script.

"Quickly!" Zicka ordered. "To the ship. I will put you ashore as close as I can to the Sunken Stones."

The Codex seemed a lot heavier than it had under the mountain, Tal thought as they lifted it over the side and on to the deck. Though possibly that was because he'd been scared to death.

They were back out in the middle of the stream when they heard the first awful screech from the mountain.

Everyone looked back. There was still a lot of dust around Cold Stone Mountain, but it was easy enough to see the thing that had made the awful, chilling call.

It was circling in the air above the mountain. A long and sinuous snake-thing with very long, thin wings that fluttered so quickly they were almost invisible. Its body was bright orange with black stripes and it had a stinger on its end.

Tal stared at it and his mouth went dry. He knew what it was. He'd seen it in the Beastmaker game. It was part insect, part reptile and could be played for Temper, Speed or Special. It was a Waspwyrm.

Tal had thought Waspwyrms were man-sized or smaller.

This one was bigger than the ship.

Somehow he knew that it had come to investigate the rising of Cold Stone Mountain.

It was looking for the Codex.

Tal hurled himself across the deck, throwing his coat over his head.

Milla had the same idea. A few seconds later, the Codex was covered by their coats. Tal was surprised to see just how smelly and dirty his coat was. He'd got so used to wearing it he'd forgotten how rank it was. He hoped the Codex wouldn't mind.

Tal looked back at the Waspwyrm. It was flying down to the point where they'd gone in to get the Codex. He wondered if it could scent them or follow their tracks.

"We'd better hurry," said Milla grimly. "Whatever that is, it looks for us."

"It's a Waspwyrm," said Tal. He felt sick. "They're not very smart, but their sting is acid and they can squirt it. They also go crazy when they fight and they're very, very fast. That one is a giant. They're supposed to be small."

"How do they stand up to lightning?" asked Milla.

"Lightning?" repeated Tal. He felt a bit better. He'd forgotten about the Storm Shepherds. "I don't know. They're sort of half lizard, half insect. I suppose it would kill them."

"Good," said Milla, and she went over to talk to Odris and Adras.

Tal kept looking back towards the mountain. He was relieved to see the Waspwyrm rise up and disappear back the way it had come instead of following him.

But he knew that something would find them

soon. They had to get to the Sunken Stone Circle and back to the Castle. The feeling of dread, the worry about Gref, was at its strongest now because they were so close. As soon as he could uncover the Codex, he could ask it the questions that were burning in his head. As soon as it answered, he would know who was holding Gref... and perhaps what had happened to the rest of his family.

Half an hour later they came to the furthest point south and east that the ship could go. After unloading the Codex, Zicka pointed out which direction the Sunken Stone Circle lay in and wished them farewell from the deck of the ship.

Milla clapped her fists together before the lizard, to give him honour, and Tal flashed his Sunstone, though guardedly in case anyone was watching from a distance.

"If ever you come to Aenir again," said Zicka, "you will find news of me, at least, at the place commonly called Kurshken Corner. It is where most of my people live. Roquollollollahahinanahbek and I wish you well, daughter of Danir and son of

Ramellan. I would like to talk to that Codex of yours, but I know now is not the time. Nor ever, I suppose, for we Kurshken are sworn never to cross to your world. Farewell!"

Without any sign or spoken word from the small green lizard, the ship turned back into the river and sped away. Tal and Milla waved once, then picked up the Codex and began to walk.

Adras and Odris, obeying Milla's previous instructions, flew above them at different heights, keeping watch.

Tal and Milla did not speak as they walked. It was an effort to carry the Codex, but that was not why they found it difficult to talk. Neither knew how to bridge the gap that had come between them. Both in their own way wanted to, but both were held back by what they were and how they had changed. Tal was not really a Chosen any more and Milla was not really an Icecarl. But they did not know how to forge a new understanding or forgive each other for the things that had happened.

So on they trudged in silence, pushing themselves as fast as they could through the black mud, crushed reeds and sudden pits of bubbling black metal that Milla called ghalt.

Finally Tal saw what he was looking for. They had come to the top of a hill and there in the valley below was a circle of stones. A strange circle, for the stones were buried so that only the very tops showed, so they looked rather like large mushrooms from a distance.

"The Sunken Stones!" Tal cried out, though he barely had breath to do so. He'd been there several times and his family had once transferred back to the Dark World from here. Escape was in sight!

Before they could start down the hill Odris called out from above them.

"Look out behind!"

Tal and Milla set the Codex down on its lower edge and turned to look.

First they saw the Waspwyrm. But it was not alone. Four other smaller Waspwyrms flew with it. And on the ground there was almost an army of creatures, running, leaping, loping and jumping down the previous hill. There were Vengenarls and Borzogs and Filjiks and all sorts of vicious things.

There was also a man running amidst the pack, a man in the Violet Robes of a high Chosen, Sunstones winking at his neck and on his hands.

"They'll catch us!" said Milla, rapidly calculating the relative distance between the Waspwyrms and themselves and to the stone circle.

"No," said Tal. "We'll fly. Odris! Adras!"

He held up one hand, keeping a tight grip on the Codex with the other.

Milla held up her hand too, but she said, "I thought no Aeniran could touch the Codex?"

"They won't," said Tal. He was already clenching his teeth in expectation of his shoulder being wrenched out again. "We'll hold on to the Codex and the Storm Shepherds will hold on to... owww!"

The Storm Shepherds had swooped down and lifted them up. Tal's arm wasn't dislocated out of his shoulder, but it hurt almost as much.

"To the stone circle!" shouted Tal. "Right to the middle! Quickly!"

26

The Storm Shepherds dropped them into the middle of the stone circle then both shot back up into the sky. They had to get above the approaching Waspwyrms to use their lightning.

Tal and Milla laid the Codex down. Milla was about to draw her sword and rush to the circle"s edge, but Tal stopped her.

"No," he said. "Lie down next to the Codex and put your Sunstone on your chest! I'll speak the Way to the Castle. You need to repeat it in your head, and concentrate on the colours."

"No!" said Milla. "I won't leave... even you... here to fight alone."

"I'll leave too!" said Tal. "But you *have* to go first. You don't know the Way."

Thunder boomed above them and lightning lit up the sky. Tal and Milla looked across and saw the Waspwyrms break formation and momentarily circle back as Odris and Adras shot lightning bolts down at them.

"The Codex has to get back!" shouted Tal above the thunder. "It's the only way to find Gref. Ebbitt will know what to do with it."

"I cannot leave a comrade in battle," yelled Milla.

"It's not a battle!" shrieked Tal. He racked his brain, trying to think of something that would influence her, and babbled, "Please, Milla. You *have* to go first. Think of your clan. They need the Sunstone. Gref... Ebbitt... my people need the Codex. Whatever's going on, it'll be bad for the Icecarls too. One of us has to get back."

Whatever Tal had said, it worked. Milla nodded decisively and lay down next to the Codex. She put her left hand flat upon it and held her Sunstone on her chest.

Tal took a swift look back at the approaching

enemy then bent down next to Milla. He raised his own Sunstone and began to speak the Way to the Castle.

Milla concentrated on his words, shutting out the crash of thunder and the distant roars and cries of their pursuers. She saw colour spring out of her Sunstone and wash back over her face. As in her last crossing, the colours provoked different sensations on her skin.

Tal's face faded as the colours spread and the sky changed colour. But before the sky blurred away entirely, Milla heard Odris cry out, behind the words that Tal spoke. "Adras! I'm going!"

The Storm Shepherd dropped faster than a stone, reaching out one cloudy hand. Milla felt it touch her just as all the colours flashed brighter and became a rainbow.

Milla blinked and was gone.

Tal stood up. Milla and the Codex had vanished, sent back to the Castle, back to the Dark World. Odris had gone with them.

Adras was still there, frantically flinging lightning bolts at the Waspwyrms. But while the

Storm Shepherd was keeping the flying creatures back, the other creatures were already halfway down the other hill.

Tal felt an almost overwhelming desire to run. There were scores of terrible creatures charging at him. They would be all over the stone circle in a minute or even less. If he lay down and tried to transfer himself to the Dark World, they might get him before the spell was complete.

But they'd get him for sure if he ran.

"Adras!" Tal shouted even as he threw himself down. "Come as low as you can!"

He was shivering, Tal discovered, his hand unable to stay still on his chest. He stared at the Sunstone on his finger but didn't even try to take it off. He knew he'd drop it if he did.

He immediately started reciting the Way to the Castle. Red light spilled out of his Sunstone as he spoke the words, the light flowing like water across his chest and down towards his legs.

The thunder stopped and now Tal could hear howls and shrieks and screeches that made his heart pound faster than he thought humanly possible. All his aches and pains were forgotten. Every tiny part of his mind was focused on his Sunstone and on the Way.

Tal spoke even faster, adding the other colours. He'd never spoken the incantation so quickly. He was afraid that he'd garble the words and end up who knew where. But he was more afraid of the creatures that were probably almost upon his defenceless body.

The rainbow started to form. Through the fuzziness of it, Tal could see Adras diving down to him, one arm outstretched. They couldn't cross until the Storm Shepherd touched him, as Adras had Tal's shadow. It was an anchor keeping him in Aenir.

As he saw the blurred shape of Adras swooping down, Tal saw a normal-sized Waspwyrm fly in. Storm Shepherd and monster met directly above his body. Adras reached down to touch Tal with one hand and bash the Waspwyrm with the other. At the same time the Waspwyrm jetted acid down from its sting.

Rainbow light flashed. Tal and Adras disappeared.

27

Tal arrived in the Dark World screaming. Acid was burning through his leg. He jerked up to look at the damage and hit his head on the coffin lid. He'd forgotten that he'd left his body in the Chosen's Mausoleum. It had seemed the safest place at the time.

With an acid burn on his leg and his head cracked on the lid, choosing the coffin seemed very stupid. Tal reached up to try and shift the lid. As always when he returned from Aenir, his body felt very heavy and slow.

"This is very strange," said a voice that was somehow under him. Tal stiffened in shock until he realised who it was.

It was Adras, who had become a shadow.

A puffy shadow-arm reached around Tal's body and joined with him in opening the lid. But the shadow went straight through.

"You... you have to concentrate," said Tal. His voice sounded strange to his own ears. It too was different from in Aenir. He was also speaking through gritted teeth as he tried to cope with the pain in his leg. "To make your shadow-flesh strong enough to interact with stone or flesh."

"How?" asked Adras plaintively.

"I don't know," whispered Tal. "Think of it being... I don't know... tougher. Imagine."

Adras reached past him again and this time the shadow-hand did not go through the stone. The lid began to slide open.

Tal dimmed the light of his Sunstone and Adras said, "What happened? I feel weak."

"Keep quiet," whispered Tal. He didn't want any Chosen who might be in the Mausoleum to hear them. "You're a Spiritshadow now. You need light to be strong."

"Oh," said Adras. Just as when he'd been a Storm

Shepherd, he didn't know how to keep his voice down.

Tal closed his eyes and tried to breathe more slowly. Any minute now, he told himself, Ebbitt will be looking down and he'll use his Sunstone to stop the pain. Any minute now. All he had to do was concentrate on breathing.

"Tal! What happened?"

It was not Ebbitt. It was Milla.

Tal opened his eyes. Milla was looking at his leg, where tendrils of acid smoke were still rising. Odris loomed up behind her, a huge Spiritshadow. She still had the look of a Storm Shepherd, but was smaller than she'd usually been in Aenir. Interestingly, small sparks of darker shadow occasionally shot out of Odris. Tal had never seen that in a Spiritshadow before.

"Acid," whispered Tal. "Waspwyrm. Get Ebbitt."

"He's not here," said Milla. "He left me a note, but I can't read it. You've got one too."

Tal lifted his head a little and groaned. There was a rolled-up scroll near his right hand. But he was too much in shock to pick it up or make any attempt to read it.

"Healing magic," he whispered again. "Use Sunstone."

"I don't know how," said Milla. She looked at his leg again. The acid had burned straight through Tal's fur leggings and eaten away the flesh underneath. She could see white bone. On the Ice, his leg would have to be cut off and the stump cauterised, unless there was a very skilled healer close by.

"Ask the Codex," Tal whispered.

Then he fainted.

Milla looked at the leg for a little longer, raising the fur. Then she went over to the coffin she'd just emerged from. The Codex was still in it. It had changed shape to fit, growing narrower and longer. But as she'd guessed, it still weighed as much as it ever had and it took all her strength to lever it out and set it upright next to the coffin that held Tal.

It was also a noisy operation. When she had it set up, Milla looked around the Mausoleum to make sure the noise hadn't attracted any attention. But the vast hall was quiet. The tiny Sunstones overhead continued to flicker like the Aeniran stars they mimicked. There was no sudden flare of bright light. Nor was there any movement among the rows and rows of Spiritshadow statues that adorned the coffins.

"Odris," Milla said softly, "keep a watch on that door over there. Adras, you watch the main gate."

Odris turned to the door. Adras rose up to his full height, easily three times as tall as Milla, and said, "Why should I?"

"Because Milla said so," ordered Odris sharply. "So there."

Adras snorted. A small lightning bolt of dark shadow came out his nose, which made him giggle.

Milla ignored him and looked at the Codex. She looked at it for a long time. It seemed to her that if she asked it to teach her how to heal wounds with her Sunstone, she was taking yet another step away from being a Shield Maiden. Or even an Icecarl.

Yet once again, there was the complex web of debts she owed Tal and those he owed her.

"I need to use my Sunstone to heal an acid burn," she said to the Codex. "Tell me how."

The silvery surface of the Codex rippled, but no

letters appeared.

"Speak to me," said Milla. She rapped the surface of the Codex with her knuckle. It felt cold, like ice, but left no mark and had no effect.

"I order you to tell me!"

The Codex shimmered, but no words came.

"Why don't you answer?" Milla said, her frustration making her voice harsh.

This time Icecarl runes did appear, dark symbols rising to the silver surface as if from some great depth.

Because you did not ask a question. You must ask me questions.

"How do I use my Sunstone to heal an acid burn?" asked Milla.

Watch and learn.

The runes disappeared and a picture swam into focus. A picture so lifelike that, for a moment, Milla thought that it was real. It showed an Icecarl girl holding up a Sunstone ring. It took her another second to realise that the picture was of her.

More runes appeared under the picture. They told her what to do and then the picture of Milla did what the runes said. Then Milla copied the picture. When she got it wrong because she hadn't read the runes correctly, the picture repeated what it was doing until she got it right.

It took some time. Milla had to stop the Codex a few times to check on Tal. He was unconscious, but the wound was not bleeding. The acid seemed to have sealed off the blood vessels, which was some small mercy.

Finally Milla was ready. She looked down on Tal and raised her Sunstone. Slowly she called up a Blue Ray of Healing. It had to be exactly the right shade and density, but she had memorised that. It looked right.

As her forehead creased in the sharpest frown she'd ever had, Milla played the Blue Ray across the wound. Wherever the light touched it soothed and healed. The flesh began to grow back.

Milla kept the Blue Ray going and started to build

a second ray, the Yellow Ray of Replacement. This was the really hard one. It would put a layer of light over the blue, building up artificial bone, muscle, nerves and blood vessels to act as temporary replacements until the real ones grew back.

The Yellow Ray wove back and forth, slowly replacing Tal's missing flesh, layer by layer.

Finally it was done. Milla let the light sink back into the Sunstone and let out a deep sigh of relief. Only then did she notice that Tal was awake and watching her.

"Thank you," he said. "That was well done. You have a knack for healing."

"I am a warrior," Milla replied, and for an instant Tal thought she was offended. But she went on to say, "It is the mark of a true warrior to be a healer too. Though that is more the way of a Sword-Thane than a Shield Maiden."

Tal sat up and gingerly felt his leg. It ached to the bone, rather like a nasty toothache, deep and constant. But he could use the leg if he was careful.

Adras helped him climb out. It was strange to feel friendly shadow-flesh again, Tal thought.

Somehow Adras did not feel unpleasant and clammy, as other Spiritshadows did.

"Didn't you say Ebbitt left a message?" Tal asked. Milla handed him the scroll that had been in her coffin and got out the one that had been in his. Tal opened both. It took only a moment to see they were the same. He read it aloud so Milla and the Spiritshadows would know what it contained.

Dear Children,

Somebody thinks I have become dangerous for certain Spiritshadows have tried to sniff me out. To draw them off your scent as well as mine I have gone down, down, down, down, down, down and then down once more, from my usual abode. Come join me there if you can. If you have the Codex, bring it with you. Trust no one, absolutely no one at all. Except me of course. I have found an Underfolk corridor from the Mausoleum that leads to one of their main stairs. If you take this way you should have few problems. Unless I have been caught using it, in which case you will have many problems. But then we all have problems.

Yours truly,

E.

"Typical Ebbitt!" groaned Tal.

"Where has he gone?" asked Milla. "I don't understand."

"The Seventh Underfolk Level," said Tal. "I think that's what he means."

He shook his head. "But I'm not going down there. I have to rescue Gref. That's the main reason for getting the Codex in the first place!"

"I think we should take the Codex to Ebbitt," said Milla. "It cannot be lost to your... our enemies."

"No!" exclaimed Tal. "I have to rescue Gref!"

The effort of speaking made him even paler. Despite

the Sunstone's healing magic he was still weak.

Milla did not answer, but her eyes narrowed as she looked at him.

"What do you mean when you say *our enemies* anyway?" asked Tal.

"Now that I know much more, I think there are bad Chosen and... stupid Chosen. The stupid Chosen are not important. Your enemies are the bad Chosen and they are enemies of the Icecarl too."

"Er, good," said Tal, but it was clear to Milla he didn't want to think about anything except finding Gref.

He looked at the Codex as he spoke. Milla caught the glance and said, "You must ask it questions. It will not speak otherwise."

Tal nodded and slowly made his way over to the strange silvery artefact. It looked a bit like a mirror propped up against the coffin. But its silver surface did not reflect anything.

It took Tal a moment to phrase a question. It all seemed to have happened so long ago. Gref climbing up the Red Tower after him, the Spiritshadow that caught him and took him back inside...

"Which Chosen is the Master of a Spiritshadow in the shape of a Borzog?" asked Tal.

Words formed on the surface of the Codex. A great list of Chosen names moving across and up the Codex. Then they stopped and one name grew larger and larger.

Nilhir Jerel-Orim, of the Third Order of the Red.

"Where are the rooms of Nilhir Jerel-Orim of the Third Order of the Red?" asked Tal. He wasn't sure if the Codex could answer this sort of question, but it was worth a try.

The Codex answered immediately with a clearly labelled map. As expected, Nilhir had rooms in the Red Levels. But strangely enough, the Codex also showed him having a room in the abandoned White Levels – quite close to the Hall of Nightmares.

That was where they would be holding Gref, Tal thought. It had to be. He stared at the map, memorising the location of the room.

29

"It is not sensible to try and rescue your bother now", said Milla calmly. "We should take the codex to Ebbitt. Then I will go to the ruin ship."

She did not mention the Ice. That was left unsaid between them.

"No," said Tal stubbornly. "I have to rescue Gref! That's the whole point! I have to look after my family. It's what my father—"

"You have not asked about him," said Milla suddenly.

A movement caught her eye and she whirled, her hand on her sword. But it was only Adras and Odris, getting used to their new shadow-selves.

They had already learned how to make themselves almost solid, and the reverse, to drift through stone. Now they were practising shooting shadow-lightning. Fortunately, unlike the real sort, it was not accompanied by thunder.

Milla waved at them crossly, pointing at the doors. They got the message and resumed their guard duty.

"No," said Tal quietly. "I haven't asked. I'm... I'm afraid of the answer."

Milla nodded, but she didn't really understand. Her parents were long dead.

"I suppose I should," he added. But he made no move to do so.

"I have made too many mistakes," said Milla. "My mistakes, since I do not believe everything is directed by some great Reckoner, and I just a piece upon the board. I should have returned to the Ruin Ship as soon as I had the Sunstone. I should not have crossed to Aenir—"

"I know, I know," interrupted Tal. "I *am* sorry—"

"You do not understand," Milla resumed. "I have decided that one more mistake will make no difference. I will help you rescue your brother. But we will have to hide the Codex here. And we cannot roam your Castle looking as we do now. And I need to eat and drink."

"We can get clothes and food and so on from an Underfolk store," said Tal. "It's the middle of the night, so if we stick mainly to the colourless corridors in the midlevel we can get across to where I think they're holding Gref. It's... it's near the Hall of Nightmares..."

Milla shrugged. Unlike Tal, the Hall of Nightmares held no particular terrors for her. She had proved immune to the Nightmare Machines, calling on the Crones to protect her.

"I hope we catch Fashnek by himself," she said, referring to the creepy keeper of the Hall of Nightmares.

"I don't," shuddered Tal. "We can't afford to start any sort of fight."

"Let's go then," said Milla. "First we eat and then we fight... or we sneak."

"We have to hide the Codex," said Tal. They walked over to it. Tal started to pick it up, but Milla didn't move.

"You must ask," she said. "The question will hunt you in your dreams if you do not."

Tal nodded. He desperately wanted to know that his father was alive, but he also desperately feared that the Codex would tell him he was dead.

"Ask!" urged Milla.

Tal put his hands together in an arch and scratched his nose. Then he cracked the knuckles on his left hand. Finally he asked the question, his voice gruff.

"Codex. Is Rerem Abitt-Erem still alive?"

Tal stopped breathing as letters swam to the surface. At first he didn't understand the answer. He had expected a simple yes or no.

What he got was *Not dead and not alive.*

"What do you mean?" Tal asked hotly.

Not dead and not alive.

Tal shook his head.

"What did it say?" asked Milla. Once again, before Tal could answer, the Codex supplied a translation in Icecarl runes.

"Codex. Where is Rerem Abitt-Erem?" Tal asked.

In the Orange Tower. Above the Veil.

Tal choked. His father couldn't be there! There was nothing up there but the Sunstone nets.

"How... how can he be not dead and not alive?"

He is the Guardian of the Orange Keystone. It has been unsealed and so he does not live. Until or unless the Orange Keystone is sealed again, he does not live. If it is sealed, he will live again.

"I don't understand," said Tal. What was the Orange Keystone?

He was about to ask another question when Odris suddenly came sliding back across the coffins, calling out in what she imagined was a whisper.

"People and shadows! Lots of them, coming here!"

Tal and Milla did not stop to talk. They picked up the Codex and slipped it into the coffin. It adjusted its shape as they pushed it down and slid the heavy stone lid across.

Then the Chosen and the Icecarl ran towards the Underfolk exit where the servant sculptors worked. According to Ebbitt there was another way out there.

They had just left the Mausoleum when a great crowd of Chosen entered. Light filled the ancient hall and many real Spiritshadows slipped in to mingle with the shadows cast by the statues on the Chosen tombs.

30

Milla had to lead Tal away from the Codex. Not because of his wounded leg, which did slow him down. Because of the news about his father. How could he be in the Orange Tower? What did it mean that he was the "Guardian of the Orange Keystone"?

As explained by Ebbitt in his letter, Milla found the small door at the rear of the tool shed used by the Underfolk stonemasons. It led down a narrow corridor to a more usual Underfolk corridor. Like all such ways, it was only dimly lit by tiny Sunstones of inferior power.

Tal recovered himself enough at this point to take the lead. He was so rattled by the Codex's revelations that he didn't mind admitting to Milla that he didn't really know much about the Underfolk's corridors and storehouses.

However he did manage to find his way to something he did know about: the laundry chute that he and his friends used as a shortcut between levels. And where there was a laundry chute, there was laundry. Dirty clothes, but what a Chosen called dirty now seemed clean to Tal after the disgusting furs he'd been wearing.

Tal chose to throw all his Icecarl clothes into a basket and got dressed in a Chosen child's basic uniform of white trousers and shirt, though these ones had blue cuffs and collars that didn't match his rank.

Milla however put on a Chosen matron's dress over her armour and furs, a huge sack of a thing in solid yellow, with tiny Sunstone chips round the lower hem. She then ruined it by cutting a long slit at each side so she could run.

As instructed by Tal, Adras and Odris made an opaque wall between the two as they undressed. Not that Milla cared. But nudity was frowned on by the Chosen and Tal had not totally gone over to Icecarl ways.

Suitably disguised, they dashed across a colourless corridor and into more Underfolk passageways. Tal got lost for a while and they had several close encounters with Underfolk, all of whom were pushing carts of food, or clothes or items made in their workshops far below. But every time the Underfolk drew near, Tal had Adras and Odris loom up and the servants would avert their eyes and scuttle past in fright. The Storm Shepherds were easily the largest Spiritshadows Tal had ever seen, save for the Empress's Sharrakor. They also looked strange, if not particularly horrifying, unlike many spiky, fanged Spiritshadows. Adras and Odris looked like puffy giants, but their size alone was intimidating.

It was a bitter realisation for Tal that he had found a powerful Spiritshadow after all, one that would have probably gained him automatic promotion to Yellow or even Blue. Only he had not bound Adras as a proper Chosen should. He had broken the law and gone to Aenir. He had given a

Sunstone and a Spiritshadow to a non-Chosen.

Strangely it didn't worry him. But he was growing more and more anxious about Gref. What had they been doing to him off in some distant chamber where no Chosen or Underfolk would ever hear a cry for help... or a scream?

"Where now?" Milla asked, breaking into Tal's thoughts. They had arrived at an intersection. The Underfolk corridor branched left and right, but there was also an open doorway to an Orange level. Orange six, Tal saw, noting the arrangement of Sunstones in the ceiling.

Close to home. His mother was not far away, on her sickbed. Lost and dreaming. He wanted to see her too.

"Which way?" Milla repeated.

Tal pointed down the left Underfolk corridor. His hand was shaking and he could not steady it.

They had to follow the Underfolk corridor and go down into the topmost Red level and then across into the White Rooms.

It took another few hours because they had to cross almost from one side of the Castle to the other. As it got closer to morning, the Underfolk corridors got busier too and Tal was sure some of the Underfolk looked at them even as they bowed. But Tal wasn't worried about Underfolk. They never spoke to Chosen unless they were spoken to. They probably wouldn't remember the strange Chosen and the large Spiritshadows.

Milla didn't share this opinion. Some of the Underfolk looked very smart indeed, and Milla was certain they would gossip. She contented herself with glaring fiercely at any who dared to glance up at her. Hopefully this would make them think twice about talking about her.

The White Rooms were different from the rest of the Castle. Long abandoned, they were colder, darker and much less clean. Dust rose as Tal led the way down one corridor, though there were halls and other corridors that seemed better travelled.

Finally they came to a vast, cold hall where no Sunstones shone in the vaulted ceiling. The upper reaches were totally dark and the only light spilled in from the three corridors that led there from south, east and west.

Tal looked around suspiciously, but could see no reason for the lack of light, other than the usual failings of the White Rooms. Since no Chosen lived here, nobody bothered to replace the Sunstones or direct the Underfolk to clean.

"The room is on the far side of this hall," said Tal, pointing to the door on the northern side. He spoke softly but his voice echoed in the chamber. "A good place for a prison, I guess. No one would come here by chance."

"This could be a trap," Milla said suspiciously. She looked around the dark hall noting the other two lit corridors and the footprints in the dust ahead of them. Unfortunately she did not know enough about tracks in dust on stone. They were human footprints… but that was all she could tell.

"Maybe," said Tal. "But Gref's over there and I have to get him out."

"There must be guards somewhere." Milla drew her Merwin-horn sword. Tal noted that its glow was not what it had been. Merwin horns faded slowly but surely, once they were cut from the heads of the beasts that grew them.

Tal made his Sunstone shed a low light and limped forwards. "Adras. Go ahead of me."

Adras complied without asking questions, for which Tal was grateful. The Storm Shepherd still wasn't bound to obey, since he was a free-willed companion.

So Tal had broken yet another law of the Chosen by bringing Adras back to the Castle.

"Sometimes some laws have to be broken to save greater ones," Tal whispered. He'd heard that somewhere, though he had the sinking feeling it might have been his enemy Shadowmaster Sushin who had said it.

They were halfway across the hall now, and the light from the corridors was distant and weak. Milla kept looking up and around, expecting warriors to drop through a hidden trapdoor or come up from a secret way.

But no one did. They crossed the Hall and stood outside the door that the Codex had said was the entry to Gref's prison.

The door looked normal enough. Like most doors in the Castle it was made of thin metal leaves riveted to a frame in overlapping lines. It had a long handle of polished bronze.

"Adras," said Tal, "can you open this door?"

Adras shrugged. He leaned forwards and turned the handle. The door did not budge.

"No," said the Spiritshadow.

"I mean break it down, or go through and open it from the other side."

"I'll do it," said Odris. She lay down and grew more translucent, and then slid under the door. A few seconds later, she slid back out.

"It's locked on both sides," she said. "I don't know how. There is no keyhole."

"Is Gref – a boy – in there?" Tal asked eagerly.

"There is something in the corner," said Odris. She sounded puzzled. "I'm not quite sure—"

Whatever she was going to say was cut off as Adras made himself as solid as possible and slammed into the door. It splintered into hundreds of individual metal leaves as the Spiritshadow slowly bulled his way through, dragging the broken frame, leaves and hinges after him.

"That wasn't that loud," said Tal hopefully.

He'd hardly finished speaking when a deep horn blast sounded above their heads, the sound echoing throughout the hall. Startled, Tal and Milla looked up at a hidden recess above the door. It contained a pulsing Sunstone and a complex arrangement of pipes leading to one huge pipe that opened out like a flower at the end.

"A wakener!" Tal cursed. "Just like in the Lectorium."

"I knew it was a trap!" Milla shouted.

Tal wasn't listening. He ran in after Adras, boots clinking on the broken metal leaves.

The room was not very big. There was no bed, no furniture at all. A single medium-sized Sunstone shone in the ceiling.

But Gref was there. The small boy hung suspended in a strange cocoon of shadow in the corner of the room. Tal could see his face, which was relaxed as if in sleep. But the rest of him was surrounded by a shape of darkness.

As Tal stepped forwards to look, the shadow moved. Gref slid down until he was sprawled on the floor. The shadow shook itself and formed into a shape both Tal and Milla recognised.

It was a Hugthing. A Spiritshadow Hugthing. A free shadow, for there was no sign of its master.

Tal backed away, his Sunstone ring raised. He had to blast it before it wrapped itself around him, he knew. But Gref was right behind it.

Adras was not so careful. He roared and stepped forwards, gripping the Hugthing by one shadowy corner. Instantly it wrapped round his powerful arm and started to squeeze.

"Odris!" yelped Adras.

Tal and Milla ducked to the sides as Odris charged into the room. The female Storm Shepherd grabbed another corner of the Hugthing.

Then they both pulled.

Tal dived under the tug-of-war and crawled over to Gref. His brother still hadn't woken up. Tal touched his face. It felt cold, far too cold to be normal.

He took Gref's hand.

It hung limp and lifeless.

Then he put his ear to the younger boy's mouth, hoping for the faint touch of breath.

There was none.

Tal slowly stood back up. He felt a million years old and tired, so tired that he wanted to go to sleep right there and then and not wake up until everything was right again.

But nothing ever could be right again.

Gref was dead.

31

The noise of the fighting Spiritshadows and the still-sounding wakener faded. The light dimmed. Tal stared down at the still form of his little brother from far away, his eyes fixed, unable to blink.

Behind him the two Storm Shepherds roared as the Hugthing split in half with a horrible squeal. Then Adras and Odris stood on the halves and ripped them into quarters, and then into smaller and smaller fragments of shadow. All these pieces flopped and rolled about the floor unable to get a grip or do anything. A few tried to join together only to be ripped even smaller by the furious Storm Shepherds and the tiny bits stuffed into cracks in the walls.

The wakener kept on blasting its single note every few seconds. In the silence between the blasts, shouts could be heard, close by. Orders being shouted. Not the surprised response of ordinary Chosen.

Milla knelt by Gref.

"He's dead, Milla," Tal said slowly. "He's dead."

Milla quickly touched Gref's throat, two fingers feeling under his jaw. She kept them there while she spoke urgently to Tal.

"There are Guards coming up the south and east corridors."

Tal didn't answer. He had totally and utterly failed. Gref's life was the price of his failure.

"We'll have to try the west corridor and fight our way out if we must," Milla declared. "Now, before they gather their full strength."

"I can't... I can't leave Gref here," said Tal dully. He couldn't think what he had to do, but he couldn't just run away. "You—"

Milla suddenly bent closer to Gref and pushed her fingers in harder.

"He's not dead!"

Tal couldn't believe what he was hearing.

"He's not dead," Milla repeated. "He's sick... or poisoned. Come on!"

Tal bent down and tried to pick Gref up, but his leg gave way. Milla had already turned to leave, but she looked back and shouted, "Get Adras to carry him, you idiot! Ready your Sunstone to fight!"

"Be careful with him," Tal instructed Adras. "Very careful."

Adras cradled the boy gently and ducked down to go through the door. As he bent down, light suddenly flared all around the doorway and on Gref"s wrist. The Storm Shepherd staggered back and looked at Tal.

"I can't go through," the Storm Shepherd said. "Something is stopping me."

Tal saw what it was. There was a bracelet on Gref's wrist. A bracelet set with Sunstones. He looked at it carefully. The Sunstones were all quite small and they had been especially put together to create a particular effect.

Gref was obviously in a more secure prison than Tal had imagined. Unless he could get the bracelet off – and it was a single piece – or deactivate the spell, Gref was trapped there.

Milla looked back in to see what was holding them up.

"Come on!" she said. "There are Guards in the west corridor now! We have to attack and punch through!"

"I can't get Gref out," shouted Tal.

"Then leave him!"

Tal looked at the Sunstones set into the doorway. There were six of them, all welded deep into the stone. He'd have to pry all six out to annul the spell. It would take too long.

"Put him down," Tal said, though he choked saying it. He pointed. "Carefully."

Adras put Gref back down in the corner.

"Go!" said Tal.

But Tal lingered a moment. He raised his Sunstone ring and a hot blue ray sprang out. It cut into the stone and with a few decisive movements, Tal carved his name on the wall in letters a stretch high.

It was a message for Gref, in case he woke up. Tal was leaving him now.

But he would be back.

Out in the hall Milla was already running for the western corridor entrance, with Odris close behind her.

Adras roared out a challenge to the Spiritshadows that were spilling out from the eastern and southern corridors, their Chosen masters close behind them.

"Die, little shadows!" roared Adras. Shadow-lightning flickered from his hands and he stretched himself to be more than fourteen stretches high. For a moment even Tal was scared and he understood why the Guards were approaching slowly. None of them – or their Spiritshadows – wanted to be the first to tangle with whatever Adras was.

To make them even less eager, Tal raised his Sunstone and concentrated on it. Red light flared in its depths and Tal coaxed it to the surface. Then he screamed a war cry and thrust out his hand.

Triple Red Rays of Destruction shot out from the stone, slicing across the darkness of the Hall, weaving together and then apart, striking stone, shadow and flesh. Sparks shot from stone, scraps of shadow flew and Guards shouted in sudden pain.

Tal ran as answering rays shot out. He was already looking away when a shockingly brilliant white light flashed and he felt its heat on his face.

"Strong!" boomed Adras, who was running at his side. "Again! Give me light!"

Ahead, Milla's sword left a trail of luminescent afterimages as she cut at the two Guards who blocked her way. Odris grappled with their thin-waisted Spiritshadows, holding one off with a raised foot as she gripped the other and twisted and twisted, as if she were winding up a top.

Then all four of them were in the western corridor and there was no one ahead. Shouts and cries and the call of the wakener dimmed behind them as they ran and ran.

"Which way?" Milla shouted as they came to the first intersection. A Guard stepped out and was instantly bowled over by Adras and her Spiritshadow flattened by a two-fisted punch from Odris.

"Not that way!" yelled Tal, as he saw more Guards coming up from the left. He turned and saw yet another squad coming from the right.

There was only straight ahead and they were running again as Tal desperately tried to remember the Codex's map. He didn't know the White Rooms and he was already a bit lost.

Besides, where could they run to?

"Guards ahead!" shouted Milla as they came to another intersection, a three-way fork in the corridor.

Tal stopped and stared. There were Guards ahead... but that was not the worst of it. Safely behind the first rank was the ponderous body of Shadowmaster Sushin, wrapped in the robes of the Deputy Lumenor of the Orange Order. He had his hideous, fanged monster of a new Spiritshadow at his side.

Sushin saw Tal at the same time. Despite his fleshy arms, his reflexes were quicker than the boy's. His hand flashed up and a ball of orange light flashed out, screeching across the forty stretches between them.

Adras tried to bat it away but the ball went straight through his palm, without seeming to touch the shadow-flesh.

It struck Tal as he was raising his own Sunstone, desperately summoning a blue shield from its sparkling depths.

He was too late. The shield formed as the ball exploded around his head. Tal felt burning fire in his eyes. He screamed and fell back, twisting his hands into what he imagined were blackened sockets.

"Blind!" he screamed. "I'm blind!"

Sushin laughed, and the Guards and his own Spiritshadow charged forwards.

The laughter stopped suddenly as Milla threw her Merwin-horn sword. It arced through the air like a golden lightning bolt and hit Sushin's left shoulder, the point sticking out of his back. He stared open-mouthed at it.

The Guards and his Spiritshadow stopped and looked back.

Sushin closed his mouth. A smile started to spread across his bloated face.

Then he started to laugh again.

It was the laugh that made Milla decide to run. She knew she'd missed his heart, that it wasn't a killing blow. But no normal man could take such a wound and laugh.

Tal had described Sushin to her and she had heard his fear. Now she felt it too.

This was no normal Chosen. His laugh made her feel cold inside – colder than the Ice.

32

"Adras, get Tal!" shouted Milla. "Then run!"

"I can't see!" Tal cried out as he felt his ruined eyes.

Adras picked him up and shoved him under his arm, and then they were running again, taking turns at random, always away from wherever they saw Guards.

Milla had the sense that soon every corridor would have Guards in it. They had to have a plan. She had to know where they were going.

The moment that no pursuers were in sight she stopped. The others almost crashed into her.

"Blind!" screamed Tal. "He *blinded* me!"

Milla slapped him hard. Then she held his hands and looked at his eyes.

"Your eyes are fine," she snapped. "It is like being snow-blind. You will recover."

"I will?" whispered Tal. He took a deep breath and then another. Blindness was the great fear of all Chosen. A blind Chosen was automatically relegated to the Underfolk, for they could not work with light.

"You will," confirmed Milla, though she wasn't really sure. His eyes did look normal. "If we get away. How do we get out of the White Rooms?"

"Where are we now?" asked Tal.

"I don't know! A tunnel!"

Tal thought for a moment, ignoring the pain in his eye sockets.

"The laundry chute," he said. "It'll be the only way between levels that won't be guarded. Find an Underfolk and make them show you the way."

"And how do I do that?" asked Milla.

"West. Keep going west."

Milla didn't answer. She just started running again.

Tal heard her footsteps, but he hadn't been picked up.

"Adras!" he shouted, panicked, sure that he had been left behind. "Adras!"

"Yes?" asked Adras.

"Carry me. And keep up with Milla and Odris!"

"Where did they go?" asked Adras, as he picked up the Chosen boy. "I wasn't looking."

Tal bent his head, exasperation fighting with fear inside him to see which would win. He was about to explode when Milla's voice came echoing back down the corridor.

"Adras! Come on!"

As Adras half slid and half ran with him, Tal cautiously felt his eyes again. Surely they had been burned? But he was calmer now, and his fingers assured him that his eyes were still there after all.

Then he found that Adras's shadow-flesh was quite cold and he pressed his forehead against the Storm Shepherd's side so his eyes were cooled.

"What are you doing?" asked Adras, and he slowed down to look.

"Cooling my eyes," said Tal. A thought struck him and he asked, "Can you still make rain?"

Adras shrugged, a movement that made him

nearly drop the boy. "I have to go puffy. If I go puffy I can't have legs. We could fly."

"No, no," said Tal. Having Adras fly in the narrow corridors of the White Rooms would be a disaster.

Then Tal heard two voices at the same time. One was obviously a Guard and the other Milla.

"There they are!" and "Hurry up! Hurry! I've found an Underfolk!"

Tal never heard what Milla said to the Underfolk because Adras didn't catch up before they were running again. He kept his eyes pressed against the cool shadow, blinking frequently.

Gradually he became aware of light filtering into the corners of his eyes and he felt a great surge of relief.

Relief that was dampened by the shouts behind... and now ahead of them.

Tal risked taking a look. He could see, but only just. His vision was blurry and full of floating specks and dots.

They were in an Underfolk passage now, barging between rows of boxes and bags that could contain anything. Milla was screaming – at first Tal couldn't understand why, and then he saw terrified Underfolk pressed up against the walls as they flung themselves out of the way. Then they had to do it again seconds later, as the Guards came charging after, their swords out and Spiritshadows running with them.

There was no sign of Sushin, for which Tal was unbelievably grateful.

"Stop in the name of the Empress!" roared the lead Guard, and he paused to project a Violet beam of light at Tal. But he had not warned the Guards behind him that he was stopping and they crashed into him just as he fired the beam. It hit a pile of cloth bags, exploding them into shredded pieces.

Fire caught and smoke billowed up, as Guards jumped over their fallen comrade and ran on. Spiritshadows spread to the outer walls and ceiling, where they could run more freely above and to the sides of their masters.

Underfolk tried to stay out of the way, in silent suffering.

"Chute!" said a voice Tal did not recognise. He hurled himself out of Adras's grasp and saw an old Underfolk man pointing at the swinging hatch that covered the laundry chute.

"You first!" said Milla. "You know the way!"

Tal hesitated then dived in. He had his Sunstone lit up before the hatch even banged. It was dark in the chute and he was afraid of what might be waiting in it for them. What if Sushin had guessed their plan?

Before he could think any more of that, Milla, Adras and Odris came after him. Milla cannoned into his back and that was enough to push him off the lip, into the actual chute.

"Whoa!" yelled Tal as he shot down the greased stone chute. This was at least twice as fast as he usually went!

Before he knew it he was already whizzing past the next level, the brief outline of light around the hatch a momentary flash. Then the chute did a sharp switchback turn and Tal was tumbled on his side, and the acid burn on his leg stabbed him with pain.

The next level seemed to pass in a second and they switchbacked again. This time Tal was almost upside down and Milla was pressed up against him, so they were like one big lump of laundry accelerating all the way down.

"Slow! We have to slow down!" screamed Tal as he pushed his feet against the sides of the chute. "Adras!"

"No!" shouted Milla. "Faster! We are pursued!"

Still Tal kept his feet against the sides, till his already worn soles were gone and his feet were burning worse than in the desert sands of Aenir.

Only then did he realise that Milla was laughing.

She laughed all the way down and was still laughing when all four shot out at the very end of the line, bouncing and crashing through stacked bag after bag of dirty Chosen washing.

As soon as they stopped, she was up and had the hatch closed and its lock turned.

"Now where are we?" she asked.

"Underfolk Seven," said Tal, looking around. "The Main Laundry."

"That was fun," said Adras. Odris nodded her agreement.

"No it wasn't," said Tal sternly. He turned to Milla and said, "And why were you laughing?"

Milla looked at him.

"My sword," she said. "It is up there, in the monster... the one that looks like a Chosen. Shadowmaster Sushin."

"So?" asked Tal wearily. Milla was still blurry and he couldn"t make out the expression on her face. What was funny about that?

"I threw it to save you," said Milla. "That means you have to go and get it back for me."

Tal's jaw dropped. He couldn't believe what she was saying. It was bad enough that Gref was still a prisoner and sick as well. And the Codex was up in the Mausoleum, where it was no use to anyone.

Now she wanted him to get her sword back?

From Sushin?

"Ha ha!" Milla laughed. She clapped her knuckles together. "Your face!"

"You—" Tal began. Then he stopped. A slow, hesitant smile began to spread across his face.

"We got away," he said. "But you want me to think that I have to go—"

"Yes, yes," laughed Milla as they kept moving.

"It is an Icecarl joke!" Tal wanted to laugh along...

but then he thought of Gref and the laughter stuck in his throat till it came out as a single sob.

There was a tremendous crash and a ringing sound as the hatch of the chute bent out and then snapped back.

Instantly Milla's laughter stopped.

"Quick!" she said. "Which way?"

Tal squinted, his heart pounding. He still couldn't see properly. Was it the third door that led out to the Lower Underfolk Cavern? Or the second?

"That way!" he said, and then he was stumbling around the laundry bags with the others close at his heels.

They were only just through the door when a Guard's Spiritshadow gingerly slid under the hatch and reared up to look around. Satisfied that it seemed safe, it unlocked the hatch.

Moments later, more Guards and Spiritshadows spilled out of the chute – stretching, grumbling and cursing. The chute was not suited to full-grown Chosen. More and more came out, and then the last two had to reach back in and help out a particularly round and heavy Chosen.

It was Sushin. He held the Merwin-horn sword in his hand and there was a great hole in his orange robes at the shoulder.

But there was no blood.

Coming soon, book four of

THE SEVENTH TOWER

ABOVE THE VEIL

Turn over for a sneak preview...

Tal and Milla were only a dozen stretches from the dock when the Underfolk noticed them. It was Crow who glanced across the water, alerted by a splash. Shock flicked across his face, but it was gone in an instant as he shouted and grabbed his spear.

"Look out! In the water!"

The other two Underfolk on the dock went for their spears as well, while the two in the water splashed in a panic to the steps. Weed went flying through the air as the Underfolk threw it aside in their haste to get weapons or get out of the water.

"Peace!" shouted Milla. "A truce!"

"Talk!" shouted Tal. "We just want to talk!"

Unfortunately, Adras decided at the same moment that he would help with a thunder shout. It broke across the water with all the strength of real thunder, drowning out everyone's words and momentarily stunning the Underfolk.

As the thunder echoed through the pool, Crow threw his spear straight at Tal. Milla leapt forwards and snatched it out of the air.

Tal fell into the water, up to his neck. But he kept his hand and Sunstone ring above the surface. Suddenly angry, all his thoughts focused on bringing forth blinding brilliance.

Light exploded out of the stone, banishing the darkness. Adras and Odris roared with delight, suddenly visible as hard-edged shadows, huge human-like figures of billowing cloud. They rushed at the other Underfolk, who threw their spears uselessly at the Spiritshadows. Adras and Odris batted them away.

It looked like a full-scale battle was about to develop when Milla shouted, using the voice that she had been trained to use aboard an iceship at the height of a gale.

"Stop! Everybody stop!"

Everybody stopped. They might have started again if Milla hadn't kept on shouting.

"Adras! Odris! Come back here. You Underfolk, stay where you are. We just want to talk! We're not Chosen!"

Tal dragged himself up from the water, pushing the weed off his shoulders. He kept his Sunstone burning bright, but deflected the light off the distant ceiling so it didn't blind anybody.

"It's them," said one of the Underfolk, a tall blond-haired boy... no... girl, who Tal suddenly remembered was called Gill. "The two we dragged up from adit three. I told you we should have killed them."

"Close it," said Crow. He was looking at Tal and Milla, but his eyes kept shooting across at Adras and Odris. He had a knife in his hand, held low at his side.

"We aren't Chosen," repeated Milla. She ignored Tal's furious look at her. She might not be Chosen, but he was and he couldn't see any point in pretending otherwise.

"No?" asked Crow. "You have Sunstones and Spiritshadows."

"I am Milla, an Icecarl, from outside the Castle. Tal... used to be a Chosen, but he's not anymore. The Chosen have cast him out. The guards are after him."

Tal opened his mouth to protest and then shut it again. Milla was describing what had happened to him in her terms, but it was still true. He was effectively an Outcast. He hadn't really thought it through before.

Crow listened without changing his expression. Even the news that Milla came from outside the Castle didn't seem to perturb him. The others shifted nervously and looked behind them to the open door and the tunnel beyond.

"We're looking for my great-uncle Ebbitt," said Tal. "An old Chosen. His Spiritshadow has the shape of a maned cat. Have you seen him down here?"

"Maybe," said Crow. Tal noticed that the other Underfolk seemed to recognise Ebbitt's name, and they wouldn't meet his eyes. It was also clear Crow was their leader and they would stand silently while he did the talking.

"Can you take us to him?" asked Milla.

"That depends, doesn't it?" said Crow.

"On what?" Tal asked. He was getting more and more angry. "Why don't you... why don't you just do as you're told?"

Even as the words left his mouth, Tal regretted them. This was exactly how he'd gotten in trouble with the Icecarls. His mind knew better, but it was slower than his tongue.

Crow stared at him, his dark eyes shining with a deep hatred.

"You're still a Chosen, aren't you?" he said, raising his knife. "Do this, do that! We're not your servants down here! We're Freefolk, not Underfolk. And you can wander around down here like little lost light puppets until the guard gets you, as far as I'm concerned!"

Tal raised his Sunstone, his mind concentrating on a Red Ray of Destruction...